THE WAR WITHIN

THE WAR WITHIN

By

BRAD NEYENS

Charleston, SC
www.PalmettoPublishing.com

The War Within
Copyright © 2022 by Brad Neyens

[TXu 2-309-661]

Paperback ISBN: 979-8-88590-520-6
Ebook ISBN: 979-8-88590-521-3

This book is dedicated to our beloved son, Matthew, my cousin, AJ, and my friend, Mike. May you all rest in peace. If you or someone you know is struggling with mental health issues, please seek help.

A special thanks to Ricky at Ross Co auto sales for helping me with the cover photo.

A special thanks to Andrea Scott for her great photography work.

CHAPTER ONE

It's Friday night, and in this small town in Iowa, that means it's race night. Phil is driving down an old back road in his 240 Datsun with his best friend Travis. Travis will be heading to bootcamp soon and is enjoying his last few days with his friends.

Phil tells him. "You know, I could always use your help with Phil's Pizza."

Travis says. "I appreciate the offer, but I'm not going to be doing all the work while you continue racing all the time with that partner of yours."

Phil turns away. "Well, if you ever change your mind, you'll know where to find me."

Travis asks him, "Do you have any idea on how you are going to get the rest of that money for Peggy's ring?"

Phil tells him, "No, but I am sure something will turn up."

Phil and Travis arrive at the street races. Phil pulls in and parks on the shoulder of the road with all the other cars except for the two that are currently racing. There are only about fifteen cars there. Most of the cars are classic American muscle cars and have people working on them.

Phil and Travis start to get out of his car, and their friend Brandon comes over.

Brandon excitedly states, "I hope you're ready for tonight."

Phil asks him. "Why?"

Brandon goes on, "I invited some new guys to the races tonight. His family bought the old Williams place. After I saw his ride, I knew he'd want an invite to the races. He might even be some good competition for you."

Phil is flattered. "Really?"

Brandon replies, "Yeah, and he likes to race for cash."

Phil asks, "Is he fast?"

Brandon shrugs his shoulders. "Well, he got me by about two cars."

Phil laughs. "So how much did he take you guys for?"

Brandon admits, "He got us both for $250."

Phil asks him, "Think he'll go for two grand?"

Brandon is surprised. "Man, that's a lot of money for you."

Phil admits, "I think it's time that I man up and I finally ask her."

Phil reaches into his back pocket and brings out a piece of paper. He shows Brandon the jewelry ad with a ring circled on it. He puts the ad back in his wallet.

Brandon realizes what Phil is trying to say. "You're trying to get money for that rock, aren't you?"

Behind Phil, the new guy Chris pulls back into the parking area in his car, a pearl white 1968 Super Sport Camaro. Phil smiles and walks over to talk to Chris. Chris notices

Phil walking up and extends his hand out for Phil to shake. Phil shakes his hand.

"Hi, I'm Phil."

"Chris."

Chris points across the way to a highly customized Jeep Wrangler.

Chris explains, "The guy over next to the Jeep is my buddy PJ. He's staying with us till he ships out."

Phil advises Chris, "That's cool, man. I hope you like it here so far. A few of the cops and I have a deal to leave us alone if we stick to the country roads out of town. So…I was told you like to race for cash?"

Chris replies, "Well, I do like to keep things interesting. How much are you comfortable with?"

Phil smiles. "How about two grand?"

Chris is excited. "Hell yeah, that's what I'm talking about! Finally, somebody with some balls! Do you mind if we let PJ hold the money?"

Phil states, "That's fine, but I want the left lane."

Chris waves PJ over to collect the money. Phil and Chris both hand their money to PJ and head to their cars. They go to the starting area where they stage the race, Phil in the left lane and Chris in the right. Phil does a short burnout and then pulls ahead to where the flagman lines them up. The flagman flashes the flashlight, and the race begins.

Both cars take off. Chris spins his tires coming off the line, and every time he shifts, he seems to lose ground. Phil notices he's too far ahead and starts to short shift and let Chris close the gap. Both cars pass the finish line with Phil winning by a car length. After finishing the race, they both slow down and head back to the staging area where everybody is parked. Phil stops back to pick up his money.

PJ is impressed. "Well, that was interesting. I haven't seen anybody beat him in a race in a long time, and with an import, no less."

Phil boasts, "I haven't lost since I partnered with Daisuke Auto."

Phil holds his hand out for the money. PJ hands it over. Chris pulls up in his car and gets out. He begins to walk over to Phil's car.

Chris calls out, "Oh, we definitely have to do that again."

Phil shakes his head. "Nah, maybe next weekend. But now, thanks to you, I finally have enough money for my girl's ring."

Chris is disappointed. "What will it take for you to race me again tonight?"

Phil explains, "I typically only allow getting called out once on race night. But I could probably use some new tires. I'll tell you what: I'll run you for another grand, but this time let's have Travis hold the money."

Chris thinks about it. "Give me a minute."

Chris walks over to PJ.

Chris whispers to PJ, "Hey, man, I'm a little short. How much money you got on you?"

PJ looks over at Phil. "Maybe $550, but you know that's all I have until I leave for boot camp next week."

Chris reassures PJ, "I got you, man. Remember that guy I told you about who I met on vacation in Mexico? Well, our little business venture is about ready to kick off. I should have some money rolling in soon. I'll pay you back double. Hey, you wouldn't happen to still have your rifle with you?"

PJ replies, "Yeah, why?"

Chris explains, "I don't like being hustled, and I want to teach him a lesson. Just make sure he doesn't finish the race first."

PJ is confused. "How in the hell am I supposed to do that?"

Chris is upset. "Shoot his tire or something. I just want to slow him down."

PJ relents. "Fine, I'll figure something out."

PJ pulls out his wallet and counts out the $500, leaving him a few dollars. He hands Chris the money. Chris turns around and opens his wallet as he walks over to Phil and gives him the money.

Phil laughs. "Damn, you must really like losing if you want another ass beatin'. Okay, let's do this." Phil hands the money to Travis and heads to his car. Chris looks over at PJ as he goes to his car. PJ gives him a thumbs-up. Prep for the race starts. The car motors are very loud, and there is a small crowd gathered. PJ is next to his Jeep, away from the race and the crowd. He reaches into his Jeep and grabs his rifle bag and starts to set up his rifle. Chris is waiting at the starting line; he looks back to see that Phil is doing another burnout. He looks over at Phil and has a little smile on his face. He knows that Phil's not going to finish the race. Phil pulls up next to Chris. The flagman lines them up in position at the starting line. He flashes the flashlight. As the race starts, PJ takes aim from underneath the cover of his Jeep. He shoots Phil's left rear tire. Chris's car takes off, and Phil's car comes out of the hole and blows a tire. Phil sees he is about to hit the flagman and swerves his car to avoid hitting him. Phil's car takes a hard left into the ditch, running into the fence along the side of the road.

All the spectators except PJ rush over to help Phil out of the car. He is unconscious and is pinned against the fence in his car. The spectators began to help to pull Phil out of his car. PJ stands up from his spot and puts his rifle away. He gets in his Jeep and drives away.

Travis yells out to Duston, "Go tell Charlie we're going to need an ambulance!"

Duston jumps into his car, a '72 SS El Camino, and drives off to get help. He sees a cop car that's in an intersection not far away. Officer Charles is sitting in his car, drinking some coffee and reading the paper.

Duston pulls up next to the cop car and honks at him. He's yelling, "Hey, Charlie! We're going to need an ambulance. Phil crashed; he's unconscious."

Officer Charles turns his lights on and drives off to help.

Officer Charles radios in for help. "I'm going to need a bus sent to Airport Road. There's been a car accident. I'm en route."

CHAPTER TWO

At a nearby casino, Carlos is sitting at a high-end poker table. Watching the poker game are his two bodyguards, Juan and Pedro. Cards are being dealt out. Carlos calls the big blind of $1,000 with the seven and eight of hearts. The man next to him folds.

The third man says, "Raise $5,000." He has the ace and king of spades.

Both the small and big blind players fold. Carlos calls the $5,000 slowly. The flop comes out; it is a four of diamonds, a six of clubs, and a five of hearts. Carlos checks.

The third man looks down at his cards. "Raise $15,000."

Carlos looks across the table at the player and slowly calls the $15,000. The dealer deals out the turn card. It is the ace of clubs. Carlos checks.

The third man says, "Raise $45,000."

Carlos looks across the table at the other player and calls the $45,000 very slowly. The dealer deals out the river card; it is the ace of diamonds. Carlos checks as he notices the other player grabbing for his chips quickly.

The third man announces, "Raise $150,000."

Carlos looks across the table with no expression on his face and states, "All in."

The third man states, "Call."

Both players turn over their hands, revealing Carlos's winning hand of the straight.

The third man is amazed. "How did you slow play that the whole time?"

Carlos calls for the pit boss for a rack to carry his chips. He looks across the table at the third man.

He states, "I put you on ace, king the whole way. I was hoping you would make your hand."

One of Carlos's bodyguards approaches him.

Juan puts his hand on Carlos's shoulder. "Sir, we need to leave if you want to get there by ten."

—

PJ and Chris both arrive back at Chris's new home after the races. There's a moving truck parked outside. Next to it is a party bus with loud music playing inside. Chris walks up and knocks on the door with PJ standing behind him. The door opens. Two strippers, Brittney and Lacey, are in American flag bikini tops and shorts as they step outside of the bus and look at Chris.

Brittney looks PJ over. "So, is this him?"

Chris agrees. "Yep."

Lacey giggles. "It's about time you boys got here. We almost started without you."

The two girls lean together and kiss. PJ looks over at Chris.

PJ looks surprised. "Man, how long have you been planning this?"

Chris laughs. "Oh, did I forget to tell you? I rented a cabin by the lake, and all our old friends from back home are going to meet us there." He reaches over and hugs PJ. "We're going to party till you leave, buddy. So, I must ask, are you ready to be all you can be?"

PJ salutes Chris. "Sir, yes, sir!"

Lacey grabs PJ's head and places it in between her breasts and starts to pull him onto the bus.

Parked down the street a little way is a nice black SUV. The headlights flash.

Chris looks over to the vehicle. "Ladies, can you take good care of my boy? I got to take care of some business. I'll meet up with everybody at the cabin."

PJ gives Chris a thumbs-up as he's getting into the bus. The driver shuts the door and pulls away, leaving Chris standing there. The black SUV pulls up. The back door opens, and Chris walks over to it and looks in. Gabriel and Carlos are sitting inside the SUV.

Gabriel points over to Carlos. "This is my son Carlos. He's going to be running things for me. You'll be reporting to him from now on."

Chris shakes Carlos's hand. "Nice to meet you. Your dad told me about you last time we spoke. I didn't think you were supposed to be here till tomorrow."

Carlos replies, "Sometimes I like to pop in early to see how things are going."

Chris reports, "The lab is all set up underneath the body shop. When do you want to start putting out product?"

Carlos taps the passenger-side front seat, and the man sitting in front hands Carlos an envelope full of money.

Carlos explains, "Start next week. I have two carloads lined up already. I will have them ask for you. You just make sure you're there for the exchange." He hands Chris the envelope.

Chris says, "I'm looking forward to this new partnership of ours."

He backs away from the SUV, and Carlos shuts the door. Chris looks at the money as the SUV drives off.

CHAPTER THREE

Phil wakes up in a hospital room with his girlfriend Peggy by his side. Her long red hair covers her face as she is crying. She sees him start to wake up.

Peggy starts yelling, "Your car is getting too fast to be racing it on the streets! I don't think we can handle you racing anymore."

Phil looks surprised. "We? What do you mean we?"

Peggy is sobbing. "I didn't know how to tell you this, but I think I might be pregnant."

Phil is in shock. "I'm going to be a papa? But I thought the doctor said you couldn't have children. Oh, baby, I love you so much!"

Peggy looks at Phil. "Well, I guess he was wrong."

He starts to cry and gives her a hug as she continues to cry.

As Phil comforts her, he assures her, "Baby, I love you. I'll be fine. It was only a flat tire; these kinds of things happen all the time. I just raced on them a little too long. Can you please go find my wallet?"

Peggy reluctantly walks over to a small closet, opens it up, and pulls out a bag with Phil's personal effects. She opens Phil's wallet to find a big wad of cash, and a jewelry store ad falls out.

Peggy questions Phil, "Where in the hell did you get all this?"

Peggy bends over and picks up the ad and looks at it.

Phil admits, "The same place I got this," as he points to his leg. His leg is in traction and bandaged up.

Peggy points out, "Was it worth it?" But she soon realizes what the ad is for.

Phil says, "Only if you say yes. Will you marry me? I want you to take that money straight to a jewelry store and buy any ring you want."

Peggy runs to his bedside crying and kisses him.

Peggy explains, "Yes, but only if you're done racing." She muses, "I hope Mr. Daisuke will be okay that you're not going to race for him anymore. Do you think we are going to have to pay him back to fix his car?"

Phil confides to Peggy, "I probably should have told you years ago, but that's my car. Mr. Daisuke gave it to me after I won that first race for him. Then he offered to make me a silent partner in his shop if I would keep racing for him. I figured, why not? It would give me more time with you and time to focus on Phil's Pizza."

A doctor knocks on the door and enters. He is looking at the clipboard with Phil's name on it. He then looks over at Phil.

The doctor begins, "Hi, Phil. The X-rays look pretty good, but those three fractures concern me. I'm worried you might have a little bit of nerve damage, but we'll just have to wait and see. Why don't we set up a six-week appointment?

We can get you set up for therapy after we get you out of that cast."

"Thank you, doctor."

As the doctor leaves the room, the nurse has Phil sign his discharge papers. She leaves the room. Peggy is sitting at the bedside with Phil, holding his hand. Phil looks over at Peggy.

Phil reminds Peggy, "We need to get going. Are you ready?"

At that moment Brandon comes in pushing a wheelchair. Travis walks in right behind him.

Travis is excited. "Are we all ready to go? I'm getting hungry."

CHAPTER FOUR

Back at the cabin that Chris has rented, there are people are shooting pool and partying with Chris and PJ. The music is loud, and beer bottles are piling up along the wall.

PJ looks tired. "Man, I really need to get some food in me."

Chris yells out, "Anybody else hungry?"

The crowd cheers.

Chris yells back, "Let's go get some food! I'm buying, guys!"

The crowd cheers louder and starts to leave the cabin.

At a local restaurant, Phil's party is all sitting at a big table. Brandon starts to stand up to give a toast.

Brandon taps his glass with a fork. "Hey, guys…"

Everybody stops talking and looks over at him.

Brandon begins, "I would just like to say congratulations to Phil and Peggy. It's about damn time. We all thought this should have happened a long time ago. And to Travis, one of the best friends that any of us could ask for, I think I speak for everybody here: I really hope you find the answers you're looking for."

Phil motions to Brandon that he would like to take a turn to speak.

Phil laughs. "I would like to thank Brandon for breaking my new pizza oven and picking up the tab here tonight."

As Travis starts to stand up, the door opens with PJ's party coming through. They are talking extremely loudly, and most of them are intoxicated. PJ grabs Chris and puts his arm around his neck.

PJ exclaims, "This has been the best party ever. Thanks, man."

Peggy looks over at Phil. "Who are those guys?"

Phil explains, "That's the guy I was racing when I had my accident. Why?"

Peggy stands up and starts to walk over to the group. Phil looks over at Travis. He is eating when Phil taps him on the arm to get his attention.

Travis looks up with the spaghetti still hanging out of his mouth. "What?"

Phil is a little stressed. "Can you please go stop her? I don't want any trouble tonight."

Travis stands up, wipes off his face, and walks over to Peggy as she is engaging in conversation with Chris. Chris is clearly intoxicated from the drinking.

Peggy begins to scold Chris. "So why couldn't you just wait to race him a second time?"

Chris is taken by surprise. "Excuse me, but what the hell are you talking about?"

Peggy starts fuming. "Oh, that's right, they said you never stopped."

Travis steps in between Peggy and Chris.

Travis apologizes. "Sorry, Chris. She's just a little mad about the accident."

Chris looks over at the table and sees Phil sitting in the wheelchair. Phil waves back at Chris.

Chris mutters, "Hey, sorry about that. After he crashed, I figured the cops were going to start showing up. So, we decided to get the fuck out of there."

Travis starts to taunt Chris. "That was no reason to not help, man. It was a bitch move, and you know it. Hell, your buddy's winch on his Jeep would have been a lot of help, but he ran like a little bitch too."

PJ hears the conversation getting heated and comes over to see what's going on. PJ pushes Travis on his shoulder. Travis pushes PJ back, and a fight between PJ and Travis starts. The two parties start fighting. The manager picks up the phone and starts to call the cops. Phil stands up from his wheelchair.

Phil yells out, "Stop it! She's pregnant. We're here to celebrate, not to fight."

The fighting stops as everybody looks over at Phil. Through the windows flashing lights can be seen approaching from a cop car showing up.

Phil instructs the crowd, "Now, everybody just sit down and shut up and let me handle this."

The crowd starts to break up as Phil sits back down in his wheelchair. Phil wheels himself toward the front door as Officer Charles comes in the door.

Officer Charles is getting a little frustrated. "Phil, now what is it?"

Phil explains, "Just a little misunderstanding. I think I have it all under control now. I'll take care of any damages."

Officer Charles starts to lecture Phil. "Let me talk it over with the manager and make sure he's okay with that. You know our deal only works if nobody gets hurt. I don't know who these new guys are yet, but you need to bring them up to speed quick. Or I'm going to put a stop to the racing."

Chris walks up.

Chris interrupts, "Look, officer, I don't know what he's telling you, but it was his girl who started this whole thing."

Phil tries to stop him. "Chris, just let me handle this."

Chris is clearly slurring his words. "Why don't you just go fuck yourself?"

He flips Phil off.

Officer Charles questions Chris, "Sir, have you been drinking?"

Chris turns and starts to puke. It lands on Officer Charles's shoes.

Officer Charles announces, "All right, sir, I've seen enough. You are under arrest. You have the right to remain silent."

Everybody watching the conversation starts to laugh. Officer Charles finishes reading Chris his rights as he begins to handcuff him.

Officer Charles continues, "Anything you say can and will be used against you in a court of law. You have the right to an attorney. If you cannot afford an attorney, one will be appointed for you."

Officer Charles leads Chris out the door and into the cop car outside.

CHAPTER FIVE

Two weeks later PJ and Travis are in the midst of bootcamp. This afternoon they are practicing shooting drills with the other recruits. They are all lined up like ducks in a row. General Holden and Master Chief Matthews are walking behind the men as they as practice. Master Chief Matthews is part of a new special unit called Tier One. Master Chief Matthews looks over at the drill sergeant and waves him over. The drill sergeant starts walking over.

General Holden asks him, "Well, do we have any shooters in this group?"

The drill sergeant gives him a salute and reports, "We have two, sir. They both meet your criteria, but they absolutely hate each other. They're both already shooting at Expert Marksman. I talked with them about your new unit, and they're interested."

The drill sergeant hands General Holden the two folders on PJ and Travis. He opens the folders and scrolls though several papers and photos as he looks at them.

General Holden nods his head. "They look good." He turns and starts to talk to Master Chief Matthews. "Well, hopefully we got your shooters. Now we just need to go find your EOD tech."

Master Chief Matthews points out, "I'm going to need a little time to retrain them."

General Holden suggests, "Why don't you run them over to the handgun range and see how they handle themselves there?"

Master Chief Matthews informs him, "Sir, with all due respect, considering what this unit is going to be doing, trust is going to have to be taken to an entirely new level. We're all going to depend on each other at some point to save each other's lives."

Master Chief Matthews pulls two quarters out of his pocket and shows them to General Holden.

CHAPTER SIX

Years have passed, Phil has married Peggy, and they have had their baby. Their son Brad completes their family. They have a home, and Phil is successful with his pizza place. Soon Brad's curious nature gets the better of him. Brad is thirteen years old. Phil and Brad are at the kitchen table, eating breakfast.

Brad looks at Phil. "Dad, what are you going to do with that car under the tarp out back?"

Phil looks out the window. "Why do you ask?"

Brad asks, "Can I have it?"

Phil tells him, "Why would you want that car? It's going to need a lot of work to get it back on the road again. You'd have to put a lot of money into it to get it running again. It's been sitting for years; even the body is damaged. Hell, you are not even old enough to drive yet. How are you going to get the money to fix it?"

Brad says, "Well, I figured I would start working for you."

Phil laughs. "What makes you think I want your help at work? I can't even get you to help at home without complaining."

Brad tries to deal with him. "What if I helped you more around the house and brought my grades up in school? I can prove to you that I can be a good worker."

Phil agrees. "Okay, but you need to see the car first. You need to see if it's what you really want."

They go outside to look at his car in the backyard. Phil pulls the tarp off from the passenger's side to show Brad. The car has a cracked windshield with a "For Sale" sign on it, and some of the body is rusted. There is a flat left rear tire and a huge hole in the smashed-in driver's side door. The car's interior is worn, cracked, and faded. Phil looks at Brad.

Brad looks unimpressed. "I don't think you were kidding, dad. This car couldn't do zero to sixty in an hour."

Phil laughs. "So you are saying you don't want it?" Phil goes into the garage.

Brad wonders, "What are you doing, dad?"

Phil grabs a gas can and jumper box. He heads back to the car and starts to pour gas into the fuel tank. Phil walks around to the driver's side and looks down at the hole and pauses. He reaches in to pop the hood release. Then he goes around to the front and opens the hood and hooks up the jumper box to the battery. He heads back to the driver's side door and gets in the car. Phil puts the keys in the ignition and his right foot on the clutch. He turns the motor over, and it keeps turning over for about ten seconds. The car starts to pop over like it wants to start, and finally it starts. The car runs for about forty-five seconds, and then the belts break. Phil immediately shuts off the car.

Brad's eyes grow wide. "Wow! It actually ran, dad!"

From inside their house, Peggy is looking out the window and sees what is happening. She starts to smile.

Brad looks hopefully at Phil. "So, can I have it, dad?"

Phil thinks it over. "I'll have to talk it over with your mom. My old partner and I would also have to work on it a little bit before I give it to you."

Brad offers, "I think mom will be happy to get it out of the backyard."

Phil retorts, "Not when she realizes you're going to need the garage to work on it."

CHAPTER SEVEN

After a couple years of working on Phil's old car, it is now drivable. Brad is now old enough to drive. Phil decides to try and teach Brad how to drive the five-speed. They are sitting in the car, and Phil is in the driver's seat.

Phil asks Brad, "You remember everything we discussed at home? Just do it exactly how I told you, and you'll get the hang of it pretty quickly. Make sure not to give it too much gas. Just try to keep the RPMs down; you're not racing anyone yet."

The car is sitting on a steep hill, facing up. Phil pulls the emergency brake and puts the car into neutral.

Phil tells Brad, "I am going to give you three shots at this. If you don't get it by then, looks like I will be driving home."

Brad is impatient. "Okay, dad, am I getting in that driver's seat now or what?"

Phil laughs. "I bet you kill it. Three times, and it will be another long ride home with me driving with my bum leg."

Brad gets out of the car first. He goes around the car and opens the driver's door for Phil to get out. Phil climbs out slowly and pauses to look at the freshly repaired hole in the door.

Phil tells Brad, "You really did a nice job with the bodywork."

Brad says, "Thanks, dad."

Brad gets in the driver's seat while Phil walks around to the passenger's side and gets in.

Phil looks over at Brad. "Are you ready?"

Brad states, "Yeah, I'm ready."

Phil reminds Brad, "Don't forget what I told you at home."

Brad is getting anxious. "Can I just go already?"

Phil says, "Okay, go."

The car jerks forward and rolls back a little and dies. Phil pulls the emergency brake and chuckles.

Brad is confused. "What did I do wrong?"

Phil tells Brad, "Not listening to me, for starters. You didn't leave your foot on the gas, and you let off the clutch too quickly. Are you ready for your second shot?"

Brad looks at Phil. "Yeah."

Phil starts again. "Put it in first gear and start the car with the clutch in. You'll have to use the heel of your right foot to give it gas and the toes of your right foot to hold the brake, and then transition your right foot to the gas while letting the clutch out. Try not to kill it this time, and give it a little more gas."

Brad nods his head. "Okay, dad."

Brad releases the emergency brake and starts the car and puts the car in first gear. Slowly he lets off the clutch and gives it gas. The car jerks forward, and he kills it again. Phil pulls the emergency brake again.

Phil runs his hand through his hair, trying not to be upset, "All right, it's your last shot."

Brad releases the emergency brake once again and puts it back in gear and starts the car again. This time the car rolls forward as intended. Brad is pressing on the gas a little too hard.

Phil yells, "That's too much! That's too much gas!" He looks over at the tach. "Shift!"

The car passes six thousand RPMs, and Brad shifts into second. The car gets a little sideways and spins the tires. Brad gets control of the car as Phil starts to yell at him.

"Slow down!"

Brad apologizes. "Okay, dad, okay." Brad shifts into third and slows down.

Phil smiles at Brad. "Well, where are we going?"

Brad shifts into fourth. "I don't know."

Phil asks Brad, "You want to go home?"

Brad shakes his head. "No, I want to drive more."

Phil laughs. "Oh, really, that's what you're going to call it? Next week I am going to have to take you on a little road trip."

CHAPTER EIGHT

The following week, as promised, Phil and Brad are going on a road trip. It's a beautiful day for driving as they are headed to the racetrack with Phil in the passenger's seat.

Brad starts complaining. "We've been driving forever, dad. Can you tell me where we're going?"

Phil explains, "There are some things that are just safer to teach you at the track."

Brad wonders, "Is that why we closed the shop and didn't tell mom?"

Phil looks at him sternly. "Yeah, and she doesn't need to know, right?"

Brad looks back at him innocently. "I won't tell her."

Phil states, "We're almost there. It's coming up on your left."

They pull into the drag strip, passing a big sign that says, "Test and Tune Today."

Phil instructs Brad, "Pull up to the booth. We need to pay the entry fee."

Brad pulls up and shuts off the car. Duston is sitting in a small security booth.

Duston doesn't look up from the magazine he's reading. "Fifteen dollars for spectators and twenty-five to race."

Brad starts the car back up again. Duston hears the motor and looks up from his magazine and sees the car with Brad driving and Phil in the passenger's side.

Duston is impressed. "Wow, it's about time you got that street beast fixed."

Phil proudly points to Brad. "It was all my boy's doing. It's all his now."

Duston explains to Brad, "Your dad and I go way back. You just let me know when you want your bottle filled; it's on me. Phil, you really need to stop by the tower and see my pops. He was talking about trying to get that street car class up and running again."

Brad looks confused at Phil. "Bottle filled?"

Phil brushes off Brad. "Don't worry about it."

Phil looks to the back of the car, where there are several pizza boxes sitting. He reaches back and pulls off the top box; it has Duston's name on the top of it. He hands it over to Duston.

Phil apologizes. "Sorry, it's probably cold, but I figured you guys might like some."

Duston smiles. "Oh, man, you're the best. My pops is definitely going to want to see you now. He almost loves your pizzas as much as I do." Duston reaches for the pizza box. "Go ahead and park by concessions. We've moved all the street cars by there."

Phil smiles back. "Okay, thanks, man. Well, what are you waiting for? Go ahead, pull up."

Brad drives toward the concessions stand. As he drives past, there is a sign next to the concessions stand with a list of the past race winners. It's labeled "Street Car Shootout." You can see on three consecutive years, Phil's car and name are displayed. Brad pulls in and parks the car.

Phil tells Brad, "Why don't you go grab us a couple drinks? I got to go see an old friend. Go ahead and watch the races for a little bit, and I'll catch up to you in the stands. Could you pop the hatch, please?"

They both get out of the car, and Brad pops the hatch. Phil walks around to the back. Brad walks over to the concessions stand, where there is a big line. Phil pulls out his keys from his pocket, lifts the hatch, and slides the pizzas over. He lifts the carpet in the back corner. He unlocks a small compartment, revealing a small nitrous bottle and some switches. He unhooks the nitrous bottle, grabs the pizzas, and walks over to the track tower.

—

Meanwhile, Brad waits in the concessions line. He passes the sign that says, "Street Car Shootout."

The concessions lady calls out, "Next! What can I get you?"

Brad steps up. "Two sodas, please."

She tells him, "That'll be two dollars."

Brad hands the money over to her.

She smiles at him. "That's a nice car you got there. We used to have one of those cars race here all the time. You wouldn't happen to know Phil, would you?"

Brad laughs. "Yeah, he's my dad. It used to be my dad's car. But she's all mine now."

The concessions lady tells Brad, "It's going to be nice seeing him back at the track. He always made racing a little more fun. Your dad could have easily gone pro with that partner of his. Maybe you can talk him into helping us out and possibly get that street car class up and running again."

Brad picks up the sodas from the counter and turns to look at the sign. He opens his soda to take a drink just as he sees his dad's name listed for the three consecutive years of 1980, 1981, and 1982. He starts to choke on the soda, and it comes out his nose. He looks back over to the concessions lady, and she nods her head in acknowledgement.

—

At the same time, Phil is walking up to the racetrack tower door. He knocks on it. Duston's dad opens the door.

Duston's dad smiles. "My boy just texted me and told me you brought pizza."

He reaches out for the pizza boxes and sets them down on the table. He then reaches for the nitrous bottle.

Duston's dad states, "Now, let's get that bottle filled and get you racing again."

He starts to fill Phil's bottle at the nitrous station next to him in the tower.

Phil explains, "It's going to be my boy racing today. He's taking over my old car. But let's not post his times. I don't want him bragging about how fast his car really is."

Duston's dad is understanding. "Sure, no problem. Did you want to use your old number?"

Phil shakes his head. "That would be nice, but I think he's going to want one of his own."

Phil hands Duston's dad a small piece of paper with Brad's information on it. Duston's dad finishes filling the nitrous bottle and hands it to Phil.

Duston's dad smiles. "I'm glad you finally decided to come back to the track. Maybe we can get you and that street class up and running again."

Phil nods his head. "To be honest with you, I do miss it, and after today I think we will be here as often as we can."

Duston's dad is looking at his logbook and starts writing in Brad's information. He turns back to Phil.

Duston's dad states, "Well, Brad's number will be 1998-SC. Hope you two have fun today, and thanks for the pizza."

He reaches for the pizza box. He opens it, grabs a piece of pizza, and starts to eat.

Phil is grateful. "Thank you."

He turns around, walks back to the car, and reinstalls the nitrous bottle. Phil locks up the compartment, pulls the carpet back down over it, and shuts the hatch. He heads over to find Brad. Brad is sitting in the front row, watching the races. Two funny car dragsters take off from the starting line. Phil walks up to him and sits down. Brad hands him his soda.

Phil turns to Brad. "Well, what do you think?"

Brad is excited. "Dad, these cars are crazy fast. Why didn't you tell me that you used to race here? I thought you only raced on the streets."

Phil tells him. "I really miss being a big fish in a small pond. Mr. Daisuke and I worked our asses off to win that street car class. Now, do you want to talk about the past or do you want to race?"

Brad laughs. "Race, definitely race."

CHAPTER NINE

Many years later, Phil is in his pizza shop using a small LP torch to brown the cheese on the pizza he's just pulled out. He cuts the pizza and puts it in a box and sets it on the counter.

Phil calls out to Brad, "Let's try to keep the toppings on this one. I don't want to hear any more complaints."

Brad rolls his eyes. "Okay, dad."

Brad grabs the box off the counter and puts it into a pizza carrier and walks out the front door. The door makes a doorbell sound as he leaves. He gets into his car and puts the pizza on the passenger's seat. He starts the car and proceeds to drive away. Brad is driving fast and having fun. Brad passes a cop car. The radar goes off, signaling sixty miles per hour. Inside the cop car, Captain Charles and a fellow officer are eating pizza from Phil's Pizza. Captain Charles reaches over and shuts off the radar as they continue to eat.

Brad turns down the street for his delivery. He pulls into the driveway. Chris is outside with his son Tom. They're looking through a parts book at a workbench in the garage, deciding what to do next with Tom's car. Brandon is disassembling a motor on the side. Chris notices Brad pulling up in Phil's car and smiles.

Chris looks over at Tom. "Let's keep it naturally aspirated for now."

Chris stands up and starts to walk toward Brad.

Brad looks around the garage. "Looks like you boys are having some fun. So, are you looking to go street, strip, or show with it?"

Tom faces Brad. "Are you ever going to get that piece of shit finished and actually race it?"

Chris looks sternly over at Tom. "Hey."

Brad laughs. "If I ever decided to race it on the streets, it's going to take a hell of a lot more than your daddy's fat wallet to beat me." He looks over at Chris. "That'll be twenty-seven fifty."

Brandon chuckles as Chris hands Brad forty dollars. Brad hands him the pizza.

Chris waves off Brad. "Keep it."

Brandon pipes up, "How's your old man doing?"

Brad looks over. "He's good." He turns to leave. "Well, you guys enjoy the pizzas."

Brad walks back to his car, gets in, and drives away. He pulls back into the pizza shop. He exits his car, walks up to the shop door, and opens it. Brad turns off the "Open" sign and sees Phil sitting in a booth having a beer. Brad starts to change out the garbage sacks in the dining area.

Phil asks Brad, "Do you think your mom would be mad if I got back into racing?"

Brad sits down in the booth with Phil.

Brad tells him, "I can't believe it's taken you this long to think about it. Every time we go to the track, all our friends tell me they still can't believe you're not racing anymore."

Phil looks at Brad. "Do you ever miss me teaching you how to drive?"

Brad shrugs his shoulders. "A little bit, but I think you just miss seeing me beat up on all of our friends at the track."

Phil admits, "Seeing you behind the wheel of my car makes me wonder how much different our lives would be if I never had my accident."

Brad challenges Phil, "Well, maybe next time we go to the track, I can race you in that new Z of yours? See if you still got it."

Phil smiles. "You really think you're ready to take a shot at your old man? You might have a chance if I change your setup a little bit."

Brad changes the subject. "You want me to bring Travis up to speed on the land that him and PJ were looking at getting? Their contractor stopped by earlier today, and he'll be able to start building a little sooner than planned. He finished up the other project he was working on ahead of schedule."

Phil nods. "Sure, tell them to hurry up and get here already. The first round is on me."

CHAPTER TEN

A few days later over in Afghanistan, PJ is driving a Humvee. He's talking with Travis about the shooting range they plan on opening when they get back home. Their bomb dog, Rex, is sitting in the back seat.

Travis turns to PJ. "Hey man, I got an email from Phil and Brad today. We got the land, and the contractor said he can start right away. We should be able to oversee everything once we get back to the States."

PJ laughs. "Hell, I still can't believe you guys talked me into partnering up with you two. I just really hope all this planning is going to pay off."

PJ fist-bumps Travis.

Not too far away from PJ and Travis, Carlos is holding a cell phone in a building overlooking a road. There are a bunch of Taliban members with him. PJ and Travis's Humvee is driving down the road that Carlos is watching. One of the Taliban members' little boys comes over to videotape the action on his phone. Chris brings the head of the Taliban over to the window.

Carlos looks at the head of the Taliban. "So, if we join in your fight against the U.S. Military, I'm only going to be willing to pay half of what we used to pay for shipments."

The head of the Taliban nods. "Yes, of course. How soon can you start? I am running low on men."

Carlos points out the window to the approaching convoy and presses the "Send" button on a cell phone. On the road where PJ and Travis's Humvee is traveling, an IED explodes on the road, overturning their vehicle. The Taliban leader smiles and shakes Carlos's hand. He waves the rest of the Taliban people around him to come over.

The Taliban leader announces, "Look and see what our friend has done."

An IED blows up on the road under the Humvee. The Humvee flips over and comes to a rest on its top.

PJ yells for Travis, "Are you hit? You hit, man? Answer me, goddamn it!"

There is no response. PJ tries to move, but his leg is caught on some shrapnel. He looks down and realizes he is wounded badly as military personnel rush in to help them. He can hear Rex barking in the background. PJ sees black before he passes out.

—

A few days later, Travis's wife, Tiffany, a CIA agent who works with PJ and Travis's unit, is sitting next to PJ's bed in the military hospital. PJ starts to stir.

Tiffany whispers to the nurse, "Go grab the doc. He's waking up."

The nurse leaves the room to go get the doctor.

PJ looks over at Tiffany. "How's Travis?"

Tiffany gets emotional.

Tiffany starts to tear up. "He didn't make it."

PJ gets equally upset at this news. "Do you think we are going to be able to manage the gun range without him?"

Tiffany tells PJ, "You go home and set up the shop. I'll be there as soon as I'm done here."

PJ sighs. "Right when I thought we were out of the revenge game, those assholes pulled us back in. Take the rest of Tier One with you."

Tiffany grabs PJ's hand and squeezes it. She stands up and turns to step out of PJ's room. As Tiffany exits the room, she runs into a large group of men all geared up for war; it is the rest of Tier One. Rex is sitting next to them; a small bandage is near his ear.

CHAPTER ELEVEN

A couple months later at the airport, soldiers are coming home from deployment. As they are exiting the plane, all are greeting their families with hugs and kisses. PJ, one of the last people to exit the plane, has Rex with him.

PJ walks over to a table, but he has trouble with his prothesis. The table is full of mostly empty pizza boxes. There is also a sign that reads, "Welcome home, all active and retired members of the military! Enjoy our 30 percent off military discount at Phil's Pizza. Thank you for your service and for keeping us all safe here at home, and God bless the fallen." PJ grabs one of the business cards off the table and puts it in his wallet.

PJ calls for a taxicab and takes it to Chris's car lot. PJ pays the taxicab driver and exits the cab. PJ and Rex walk in the front door. PJ is greeted almost immediately by a salesman.

Ricky shakes PJ's hand. "Hi there! My name is Ricky. Just let me know if you see anything you want to take for a drive."

PJ informs him, "I'm here to pick up my Jeep. I ordered it online last week. Also, could you go and see if Chris is available? Just tell him it's PJ."

Ricky realizes that he's a customer who's already spent a lot of money on a Jeep and had it highly modified. "So, you're the one who ordered all those parts for the Jeep. We have had our techs working on it for the last three days. I'll go see if he's available."

The salesman turns and walks away as PJ pulls up a chair and sits down at a small table. Chris is standing in front of his office with two sexy women. They are laughing and giggling while one of them is playing with Chris's tie. Chris starts to open the door as the salesman rounds the corner. He sees it is probably not a good time to talk to him. The salesman turns around as one of the lot attendants walks by.

Ricky asks him, "Hey, can you grab the keys to that Jeep we modified and bring it around to the front? The guy's here to pick it up."

The lot attendant agrees. "Okay, give me about five minutes."

Ricky stops at a file cabinet on the way back and pulls out some paperwork for PJ to sign. He walks back to the front where PJ is sitting.

Ricky shows PJ the papers. "I just need a few signatures, and she's all yours. Can I see your ID, please?"

Ricky puts the paperwork down on the table for PJ to sign. PJ pulls out his wallet and hands him his military ID. The salesman looks at it.

Ricky smiles. "Thank you for your service."

PJ asks, "Did you tell Chris I'm here?"

Ricky hesitates for a moment. "I just saw him heading into a meeting. Can I have him give you a call when he gets out?"

PJ agrees. "Yeah, that'll be fine."

PJ's new Jeep pulls up out in front of the building. The lot attendant gets out and walks in the front door. He hands the keys off to Ricky.

Ricky looks at PJ. "Here is your ID back and the keys to your new Jeep. We should have your plates in a few weeks."

PJ politely states, "Just make sure Chris calls me."

Ricky promises, "I will. Now let's go look at your new Jeep. We can make sure everything is to your liking and get you on the road."

—

The following night, Brad is napping on the family couch. His phone starts to vibrate. A text message from his friend Josh comes across the phone: "You're going to the races tonight, right?" Brad shuts off his phone and resumes trying to sleep. The home phone rings. Brad gets off the couch and answers it. Phil is in the hallway passing through and overhears the conversation.

Brad sleepily answers, "Hello."

Josh doesn't realize it's Brad. "Hey, Phil. Is Brad there?"

Brad laughs. "Hey, dummy, it's me. It's been a long day, man. What do you need?"

Josh asks, "So are you coming to the races tonight?"

Brad sighs. "No, I'm not really feeling it, man. I had a sixteen-hour day today."

Josh explains, "I heard Tom was going to be there because he finally finished his car."

Brad starts to get excited. "Let me call Rachel and tell her I am going to go racing tonight."

Josh laughs. "All right, man. I'll see you there."

Brad grabs his phone and turns it on. He calls Rachel. She answers quickly, "Hi, baby."

Brad asks her, "You don't have anything planned for us tonight, do you?"

Rachel offers, "I was just going to bring some movies over."

Brad tells her, "I thought I would go to the races tonight instead of hanging out. Is that okay?"

Rachel is a little disappointed. "I suppose I can catch up on my schoolwork, then. Have fun, baby. I love you."

Brad reminds her, "I love you more."

Brad heads outside to his car. The exterior has now been fixed up and painted a deep blue. On the driver's and passenger's sides are the Phil's Pizza company logo. He starts the car and backs out the driveway. Brad is one of the last people to arrive at the street races. His phone starts to ring.

He answers using his hands-free phone in his car. "I'm just pulling in now, man."

Josh is talking fast. "Tom is talking shit about how easy kicking your ass will be. You need to shut his ass up."

Brad instructs Josh, "Tell him it's a grand or no race."

Josh thinks that is interesting. "That's funny. He said something about wanting to race you for some serious cash or he wasn't going to waste his time. I don't even know if he has finished tuning it."

Brad informs him, "Brandon built and tuned his car. I'll guarantee he's fast."

Brad pulls to the starting line just as the cops pull in to break up the races. Everyone starts to leave. Tom pulls up next to Brad in his '69 Camaro.

Tom is yelling at him over the car noise, "Hey, we're not done yet. I'm headed out to Airport Road. Let's finish this!"

Brad agrees. "Okay, I'll see you there in a little bit."

The light changes, and Brad heads right and Tom heads left. Brad calls Josh on his hands-free phone.

Brad tells Josh, "We're going to head out to Airport Road to finish this."

Josh is confused. "What's up with Tom? Why does he want to race you so bad?"

Brad explains, "My dad driving this car is the only thing that's ever beaten his dad in a street race."

Brad hangs up with Josh and continues driving. His phone rings again.

Brad sees that it's his dad calling. "Hey, dad. What's up?"

Phil asks Brad, "Are you racing?"

Brad is frustrated. "Come on, dad. You know me better than that."

Phil agrees. "Yeah, I do. Why do you think I broke up the races?"

Brad is upset. "Why would you do that, dad?"

Phil explains, "I didn't send you on that delivery to settle my old scores."

Brad tells him, "There's a grand on the line here, dad. You know he's going to be some easy money. You know there's no way he's going to outdrive me on these streets."

Phil relents. "All right, but you don't race him till I get there."

Brad informs him, "Okay, we're heading out to Airport Road now. I'll let him know as soon as I get there."

Brad hangs up the phone and pulls into the parking lot next to a golf course where Tom is waiting for him. He calls out to Tom as he gets out of his car.

Brad says, "I can't race till my dad gets here."

Tom laughs. "My dad said that this was probably going to happen."

Tom pulls his phone out of his pocket and starts to call his dad as Josh pulls in. Josh gets out of his car and walks up to Brad.

Josh wonders, "What's going on, man? Let's get this show on the road."

Brad tells him, "My dad said I can't race him until he gets here."

Josh is surprised. "What? Come on, man."

Brad shrugs his shoulders. "I told you before. My dad doesn't want me racing on the streets. He's on his way."

Josh says, "All right. I heard it running earlier, and it has a pretty big cam. He was bragging that he has to run race fuel to keep it running right."

Brad nods. "Thanks for the heads-up, but I am pretty sure this race is not going to happen tonight."

Phil shows up in a brand new, highly modified 2023 Nissan Z and walks directly over to Tom. Phil hands him two thousand dollars.

Phil looks at Tom. "Tell your dad we're even and to find a new place to order pizza."

Tom states, "My dad said you would probably do something like this, and he is on his way. He wants to talk to you."

Chris shows up in a nicely maintained '68 Camaro. He stops in the middle of the street where the races start instead of where everyone is talking. He shuts off the car and starts to walk over.

Chris calls out to Phil, "It only took twenty years of ordering pizza to finally get you and that car back on the streets."

Chris sees Tom holding a wad of cash. He holds out his hand to Tom for the money. Tom hands the money back to Chris.

Chris points to Brad as he looks at Phil. "Is he as good as you?"

Phil boasts, "Better. Brad will take the left lane."

Both men turn to walk toward the cars. Phil motions to Brad.

Phil tells him, "I'm going to let you finish my race tonight. You're going to be racing Chris tonight. He's not one of our friends, so no games with this one. No lifting. It's probably got a few extra horses under the hood since last time. You will have to slide the clutch a little more than you usually do. Give it about fifteen feet before you are all the way out. Now, let me see your keys."

Brad looks at him. "I want the left lane."

Phil lets him know, "Yeah, I got you the left lane."

Brad and Josh exchange glances before they start to look on as he hands Phil his keys. Phil goes around to the hatch. Using Brad's keys, he unlocks the hatch, lifts it up, and picks up the back carpeting to reveal a small compartment inlaid into the frame. Using his keys, he unlocks and opens the compartment, where there is a small nitrous oxide bottle, a two-stage boost controller switch, and a rev limiter switch.

Brad stops him before he turns the valve and switches. "Dad, I don't think I'm going to need the nitrous."

Phil disagrees. "You're going to need it. He's got a lot more motor than you do. There's no need to keep it close."

Phil turns the valve on the small nitrous tank and flips two switches in the compartment. He shuts the compartment and the hatch. He heads over to the right-side tire, leans down, and, using a handheld tire gauge, releases some air from that tire. Then he goes to the left side to release some air from that tire. Phil opens the driver's door and sits down. Phil puts Brad's keys in the ignition.

Brad asks him, "What were the two switches, Dad?"

Phil tells him, "I'll answer all your questions when you get home tonight."

Phil turns the key to the "On" position and adjusts the aftermarket tach to 9,400 RPM. Phil gets out of the car. He puts his hands on Brad's shoulders. Phil looks him right in the eyes.

Phil instructs Brad, "No short shifting. You're going to be shifting 9,400 now. You might have to backpedal it a little till you are used to the extra power. Come out of the hole like you do at the track. Remember, these are your streets. You drive them every day. I beat him years ago, and I know you can too."

In the background, Josh is pulling out his phone, getting ready to film the race. Brad gets into the car and starts it. Before he gets to the starting line, he does a short burnout. Chris does not do a burnout and stops at the starting line.

Tom's girlfriend lines Brad and Chris's cars up. She takes two steps back, then flashes the flashlight, and the race begins.

Chris comes out of the hole spinning. Brad comes out of the hole hard. Brad's car pulls three car lengths ahead. The shift light flashes from the tach in Brad's car. Brad shifts into second. Chris shifts and loses ground, about half a car length. Brad's shift light flashes, and he shifts into third. Chris shifts into third and gains two cars. They both cross the finish line with Brad winning the race. They both pull back into the parking area. Brad gets out of his car. He walks over to Phil, who is leaning on his Nissan Z.

Brad is shocked. "What the hell was that, dad? It's never pulled that hard."

Phil tells him, "I said we will talk about it when we get home."

Josh runs up.

Josh is excited. "Wow, man, what was that?"

Brad looks at Josh. "I know!"

Chris pulls in next to Phil and hands him the cash. Phil takes it.

Chris looks at Phil. "How did you know after all these years that your old car would still beat me?"

Phil shrugs his shoulders. "I didn't. I knew my son's driving would."

Phil opens the door of his new Z and gets in as Chris speeds away. Tom follows.

CHAPTER TWELVE

Brad and Josh go back to Brad's house. Josh gets out of his car and walks up to Brad.

Josh looks at his phone. "Hey, I got to take off. My girl just texted; she wants me to come by. Fill me in tomorrow. I want to know what your dad did to your car. Just to give you a heads-up, I posted a video of your race. It's already getting a shit ton of views."

Brad sarcastically says, "Great. I'm sure my dad's going to love that."

Josh leaves, and Brad goes into the house. Peggy has a headset on and is listening to music while running the vacuum. She pulls off her headset. She greets Brad as he walks in, and she shows off her freshly painted fingernails to Brad. They are a deep purple.

Peggy smiles. "What do you think? I just might have a new favorite color. I was going to make some popcorn; would you like some?"

Brad shakes his head. "No thanks, mom, but I do really like your new color."

Brad sits down at the table with his dad. Peggy puts her headset back on and continues to sing and dance. She vacuums a little more and then puts the vacuum in the hall closet. Peggy goes into the kitchen. She puts a package of popcorn in the microwave and starts it. She reaches into the cupboard to grab a bowl.

Phil is talking to Brad. "That's the last time I want you racing on the streets."

Brad is frustrated. "Hang on there, dad. It's my car now, and if I want to go racing with it, I'm going to do it."

Peggy pulls her headset off.

Peggy looks surprised. "Did I miss something? You're not street racing again, are you?"

Phil looks over at Peggy. "No, he was."

Peggy gets upset. "You never told him, did you?" She storms out of the room.

Phil looks back over to Brad. "So, this is the point in your life where you decide to make all your own decisions that could get you hurt."

Brad says, "It's not like that, dad."

Phil explains, "I shut off the rev limiter that Mr. Daisuke and I installed before we gave you the car. I also turned on your second stage of boost. Your car makes power all the way up to 9,800 RPMs."

Brad smiles. "So, what you are saying is I outdrove him?"

Phil laughs. "I always knew you were the better driver, and you know these streets almost as well as I do."

The microwave beeps. Phil stands up and grabs the bowl off the table. He removes the popcorn from the microwave and starts to pour it into the bowl.

Phil looks over at Brad. "Now, I better go smooth things over with your mom. One of these days you're going to realize there's more to life than that car. Are you ever going to man up and ask Rachel to marry you? If you know she's the one, why wait?"

Brad looks down. "I'm just nervous, dad. She might say no."

Phil asks Brad, "You love her?"

Brad says, "Yeah…"

Phil asks, "Do you think she loves you?"

Brad nods. "Yes."

Phil tells him, "If you are worried about money for the ring, just take it out of the business account." Phil grabs the popcorn bowl. "I should talk to Mr. Daisuke about you possibly driving for him." Phil walks out of the room, carrying the bowl with him. Phil calls out, "Honey?"

After Phil leaves the room, Brad reaches into his pocket and pulls out a ring box. He opens it up and looks at the ring inside.

CHAPTER THIRTEEN

It is the following night, and it's raining. Phil is cutting up some pizzas and placing them in boxes.

Phil calls over to Brad, "I know we don't usually deliver out that far, but it's a pretty big order, so I told him you would. I'll start the cleanup."

Brad is putting pizzas into pizza carriers. "Man, these guys better tip big. I will definitely need some extra gas money for this one."

Meanwhile PJ is driving his brand new, highly modified Jeep, and it's lightly raining. He pulls into the land that is under construction that he and Travis purchased. He parks directly in front of a big sign with a picture of Travis and PJ that says, "Coming Soon: Tier One Tactical Firearms and Shooting Range, owned and operated by Travis and PJ. We have a combined forty years of combat experience."

PJ gets out of his Jeep. He has been drinking heavily; he has a fifth of hard alcohol in one hand and a Sig Sauer handgun in the other. Rex starts barking. Stumbling, PJ walks out in front of the Jeep with the lights on by the sign and looks up at it. Slurring his words, he begins to talk to Travis's picture on the sign.

PJ says, "We had a pretty good run, didn't we? After all the shit we've seen. You weren't supposed to go out that way, man. Why'd you let me drive that day? You dumb son of a bitch. You should be here, not me."

He raises his sidearm to the sign and unloads the mag into it. He finishes off the bottle of alcohol and throws it at the sign. He falls. He picks himself back up, goes to the driver's side door of the Jeep, and gets in. He puts his Jeep in gear and runs over the sign. PJ starts to do doughnuts on the land. Rex starts barking. He starts to get out of control and crashes into the ditch by the street.

PJ looks down on the seat where he placed the sidearm. He starts fumbling around in his backpack that is on the passenger's seat, trying to find a new mag. He picks up the new mag and loads it. At that moment he sees some headlights coming down the old country road. It's Brad coming back from his delivery. Brad sees the Jeep in the ditch. He starts to slow down to see what's going on. Brad pulls over and stops. He gets out of his car and walks over to the Jeep.

Brad calls out, "Hey, are you all right? PJ, is that you? I almost didn't recognize you in street clothes."

PJ looks over at Brad through the open window of the Jeep. He has the gun in his left hand. Rex starts to bark. Brad notices the handgun.

PJ tells Brad, "I don't need any help. Get out of here."

Brad is concerned. "Sorry to hear about Travis."

PJ says, "Thanks, I appreciate that, but I need you to leave. You're not going to want to see this."

Brad offers, "Whatever's wrong, it's not worth doing that."

PJ yells at Brad, "JUST FUCKING LEAVE!"

PJ raises his sidearm to his head and has his finger on the trigger. Brad reaches in and puts his finger behind the trigger, preventing the trigger from being able to be pulled.

Brad pleads with PJ, "Let's just get you sobered up."

PJ says, "No, just fucking leave."

PJ tries to pull the trigger. Brad's finger will not move.

Brad winces in pain. "You can break it, but I am not going to let you be one of the twenty-two today."

PJ squeezes the trigger. Brad groans in pain a second time.

Brad begs, "Please, let's just get you sobered up."

PJ looks over at Brad's car and sees the logo on the door.

PJ says, "Well, I definitely could go for a few slices of your dad's pizza."

Brad points over to Rex. "So, this must be Rex. Travis said he was coming up for retirement soon, and he was hoping that you guys could bring him home."

Brad takes the gun from PJ and puts it behind his back under his belt. He starts to help him out of the Jeep. Brad reaches down and pets Rex as he jumps out of the Jeep.

PJ looks at Rex. "Rex, get in the car." He turns to Brad. "I've been wanting to talk to your dad since I got back."

PJ opens the door to Brad's car. Rex jumps in and finds a seat underneath the back window.

Brad tells him, "Well, you guys will have plenty of time to catch up when we get there. What kind of pizza would you like?"

PJ shrugs. "I don't care. Any pizza from your place would be great."

Brad pulls out his cell phone and calls his dad as he gets into the driver's seat.

Brad asks him, "Hey, dad, can you throw a house pie in, please? I'm going to be bringing PJ by. He says he would like to talk to you."

Phil sounds happy. "Great, it would be good to finally see him."

PJ gets into the passenger's seat. Brad starts the car and drives off.

———

Back at the shop, Phil is pulling the pizza out of the oven. He then uses the small LP lighter to brown some of the cheese and starts to cut it up. Brad, PJ, and Rex come in through the front door. Brad grabs the garbage by the front door and goes to take it out the back door.

PJ walks over to a booth and goes to sit down. He has a little bit of trouble with his prosthesis, and Phil notices that. Phil, with his slight limp, walks over to sit down across from PJ.

Phil points to PJ's leg. "How's your leg?"

PJ states, "It fucking sucks."

Phil says, "It'll get better, man. It's great to see you again. Hell, has it really been over twenty years? I just wish Travis was here. He was like a brother."

PJ agrees. "Me too. Travis really wanted to be here when I told you."

Phil looks confused. "Tell me what?"

PJ quietly tells Phil, "I might've had a little something to do with your accident."

Phil is confused. "What the hell are you talking about?"

PJ explains, "The night of your accident, I shot your tire out. I was just supposed to slow you down."

Brad comes in from the back door after taking out the garbage. He walks over to the sink and starts to wash his hands. He grabs the pizza that Phil cut up off the counter. He starts to walk over to the cooler to grab a bottled water.

As Brad reaches into the cooler, Phil reaches across the table and strikes PJ in the face. A fight ensues. Brad puts the pizza back down on the counter and starts to break up the fight. Rex starts barking.

Brad yells, "If I wanted to see two cripples fight, I would have made popcorn."

Phil is clearly upset. "Can you close the shop tonight? I can't fucking deal with him right now."

Brad pats his dad's back. "Yeah, okay. I got it, dad."

PJ tells Phil, "I'm going to make this right, man."

Phil's back is turned to PJ as he walks out the door.

Brad looks over at PJ. "You need to tell me what you said to my dad to piss him off so much."

PJ is rubbing his cheek. "Damn, your pops has one hell of a right cross. Why don't we sit down, and I can explain?"

PJ starts to sit down in a booth. Brad hands PJ the freshly boxed-up pizza off the counter and sits across from PJ. Rex sits down next to PJ.

PJ opens the pizza box and starts to explain. "Well, to make a long story short, I caused your dad's car accident." PJ takes a bite out of the pizza.

Brad is surprised. "I take that back. Maybe I don't want to know. I'm sure he'll forgive you; just give him some time. Why don't you eat a few slices and sober up a bit? I'll go grab you a water. Then we can go see about your Jeep."

Brad gets up to get the water. He opens the cooler, grabs a water, and tosses it over to PJ. PJ misses the catch, and the bottle hits PJ in the chest.

Brad laughs. "Damn, how much did you have to drink?"

—

Back at Phil's house, Phil opens the garage door and walks over to his workbench. The tires from his old car are underneath it. He pulls out the tire that was blown and looks it over carefully. He notices a small hole in the middle of the inside of the wheel. Phil starts to get mad. Peggy walks into the garage.

Peggy looks at him. "What's wrong? Are you thinking about your accident again?"

Phil, with a tear running down his cheek, tells her, "It wasn't an accident."

Peggy embraces Phil.

CHAPTER FOURTEEN

The following day Phil pulls into Chris's car dealership and parks right next to Chris's '68 Camaro. Phil keys the full length of Chris's car a couple times. He then walks to the back driver's side tire, pulls out a pocketknife, and pops the tire with it. When he is finished, he stands back up, and there is a crowd of people that just came out of the front of the building. Chris and Carlos are some of the last people to see what is going on outside and come out of the building.

Chris calls out to Phil, "Okay, now you have my attention. Can you please stop destroying my fucking car?"

Phil walks up to Chris. "Oh, we're not even close. You having PJ shoot out my tire cost me more than you will ever know."

Chris looks surprised. "What the hell are you talking about?"

Phil leans in and whispers into Chris's ear, "PJ stopped by last night, and he told me everything."

Chris realizes what Phil is saying. While Phil whispers in his ear, he pulls out a small collapsible billy club, snaps it open, and hits Chris in his left knee. Chris immediately falls to the ground and grabs his knee. Phil starts to walk away, stops, turns back, and notices people starting to call the cops.

Phil tells Chris, "I go to jail over this, and you're going to make one hell of a cellmate."

Chris looks over and sees what's going on with the crowd.

Chris tells the crowd, "Put your phones away! It's just a couple of old friends settling a bet. Now, can somebody go get me a bag of ice?"

As Phil walks past Chris's car, he shatters the driver's side window on the way to his Z.

As Chris lays on the ground, he mutters, "Really?"

Phil flips him the bird as he continues to walk away.

Carlos and his two bodyguards come over to help Chris up off the ground.

Chris yells, "Hurry up with that fucking ice!"

Chris is now standing up with the support of Carlos's two bodyguards. One of Chris's employees comes running out with a bag of ice. Phil gets in his car and drives away.

Juan asks Chris, "You want us to take care of that for you? We have some downtime while we are waiting for the next load to be finished."

Chris is in pain. "I think I would like that. Yeah, fuck him up pretty good, but do it at Phil's Pizza."

CHAPTER FIFTEEN

A few days later, Phil is walking up the driveway after getting the mail out of the mailbox. He passes Brad's car and drops a piece of mail. Phil bends down to pick it up from under the car. He sees a small puddle of coolant on the ground. Brad comes out the front door in a hurry and sees Phil by the car.

Brad tells him, "Josh and I should have the new security system up and running by the time you and mom come in."

Phil smiles. "That would be nice. Hey, when was the last time you checked your fluids? I think you might have a leak."

Brad starts to say, "I just checked them last night before I went…"

Phil finishes for him, "Racing?"

Brad laughs. "Come on, dad. You really can't still be mad."

Phil explains, "It's not that I'm mad. I just don't want you to get hurt. Why don't you take my car today, and I'll see what's going on with yours?"

Phil throws Brad his keys. Brad catches them.

Brad smiles. "Thanks, dad. I hope you guys really like your anniversary present. It's nice that you're going to finally let me do some upgrades around the shop."

Brad gets into Phil's car, starts it, and drives away. Phil opens the hood and starts to look around at the motor. He finds a small crack in the side of the engine block. He touches the fluid seeping out and rubs his fingers together. He smells his fingers. Phil pulls out his wallet from his back pocket and takes out an old business card. He shuts the hood and walks back inside the house. He goes straight to the phone hanging on the wall and starts to dial the phone number on the card. The phone starts to ring on the other end.

~

A few states away, inside Mr. Daisuke's shop, the phone rings.

His secretary answers the phone. "Daisuke Auto. How may I direct your call?"

Phil asks, "Mr. Daisuke, please."

Mr. Daisuke's secretary says, "May I tell him who's calling?"

Phil jokingly tells her, "Just tell him I'm really enjoying the new Z."

Mr. Daisuke's secretary is surprised. "I'm sorry, Phil. I didn't recognize your voice; it's been such a long time. He's really looking forward to talking to you. You know he's probably going to try to get you to drive for him again."

Phil laughs. "Let me guess: his new driver is not working out again."

Mr. Daisuke's secretary states, "Yes, he's very frustrated. One moment and I'll transfer you."

—

Mr. Daisuke is in his garage, tuning a car that's running on the dyno. He's sitting at a desk next to the car with a laptop. He's tuning the car as they are doing the dyno run with the car. The phone rings with a red light flashing. Mr. Daisuke sees this and motions with his hand across his throat to shut it down.

Mr. Daisuke yells, "Shut it down, guys."

Mr. Daisuke pulls out his ear protection and puts on his headset to answer the phone.

His secretary says, "I have Phil on the line for you."

Mr. Daisuke is excited. "Yes. Put him through."

His secretary sends the call through.

Mr. Daisuke smiles. "Phil, it's been too long, my old friend. Please tell me you're calling to say you will drive for me again. My driver that I have now just doesn't push my cars the way you do."

Phil starts, "I wish, but I…"

Mr. Daisuke groans. "Oh, come on. You at 90 percent is better than my current driver on his best day. Why don't you fly out here tomorrow and you can show him how a real driver does it?"

Mr. Daisuke's mechanic and driver Lee looks over from behind the wheel of the GT-R on the dyno and gives Mr. Daisuke a puzzled look.

Mr. Daisuke explains, "I can fly you back when we are done. I really can't stand losing anymore, and I would love for you to drive for me again. Also, I think it's time I cash you out. I think you'll be extremely pleased with your buyout."

Phil states, "Sounds to me like he doesn't have the faith in your cars that I do."

Mr. Daisuke is pleased. "It's settled, then. I'll see you tomorrow. We'll have a fun day at the track and can catch up then."

Phil confirms, "Okay, I'll move my schedule around. I'll see you tomorrow."

Mr. Daisuke admits, "You have no idea how happy this makes me. If you need anything, just name it."

Phil tells him, "We can talk about that after I'm done driving for you."

~

Peggy walks down the hallway and sees Phil. She smacks his ass as she is heading to the kitchen. "Hey, sexy."

Phil turns and looks at her as he hangs up the phone.

Phil is smiling. "Hey, babe, I'm going to go drive for Mr. Daisuke for a couple of days."

Peggy sighs. "I knew you accepting that new Z had some strings attached to it, didn't it?"

Phil tells her, "Honey, it's not like that. I called him. Brad's car is probably going to need a new engine. And would it really be such a bad thing if I started racing again?"

Peggy grabs him and pulls him close. "No, I think you should have done it years ago. It's kind of selfish of me to get mad at you for doing something you love. You put that part of your life on hold for us. I think we can handle running Phil's Pizza if you want to get back into racing."

He picks her up and starts to carry her down the hallway toward their bedroom.

Peggy starts to giggle as she is being carried. "Don't we have to open up soon?"

Phil tells her, "Brad can handle it."

Phil shuts the door behind them as they go into the bedroom.

—

Meanwhile, back at the pizza shop, Brad pulls up in Phil's car. Josh is leaning against his car. Brad starts to get out.

Josh is pointing to his watch. "You know you're like thirty minutes late?"

Brad agrees. "I know, sorry. Let's just get this done."

Josh looks over at Phil's car. "Why are you driving your dad's car?"

Brad explains, "My dad noticed I had a leak. He's going to look at it for me while we're working on installing the new security system. I'm going to have to give you a ride in my dad's car too. I can't believe how fast this thing is."

Josh jokingly states, "Obviously, not fast enough; your ass was still late. Let's get started." He pulls the box out from inside his car. "Man, this thing does everything. You know you can even stream the video to your phone? It even backs up to my private server. This is the best one I sell."

Josh and Brad start walking up to the door. Brad unlocks and opens it. As the door opens, it makes a doorbell sound.

Brad looks at Josh. "What would you think if I proposed to Rachel next week at the party?"

Josh, with the box of the new security system parts in one hand, pulls out his phone with his free hand.

Brad is confused. "Who are you calling?"

Josh, laughing, says, "Amanda, to tell her we're not going to the party now."

Brad laughs. "Why?"

Josh explains, "I don't want her getting her hopes up after seeing you give Rachel that ring you've been carrying around forever."

Brad tells him, "Then how are you going to handle the wedding, cause your ass is going to be my best man, right?"

Josh relents. "All right, but I'm going to throw you one hell of a party."

Josh puts his phone back into his pocket. He embraces Brad.

CHAPTER SIXTEEN

Phil and Mr. Daisuke are in his private jet with it taxiing to a parking spot. They are having some drinks.

Mr. Daisuke is toasting Phil: "I'm so glad you're finally going to drive for me again. Did you see the look on Lee's face when every lap you had was better than his best time? It was absolutely priceless."

Phil tells him, "I really enjoyed the way the GT-R handled for me. I can get a little bit faster once I get more comfortable with it."

Mr. Daisuke smiles. "Now that's what I like to hear. Do you remember when I told you I was going to cash you out? Take this, and just remember I'm pretty good at what I do too."

He hands a check over to Phil. Phil looks at the check.

Phil's eyes widen. "I knew you were making good money on those races, but damn…"

Mr. Daisuke stops him. "No buts. You helped me grow Daisuke Auto to where it is today. Your boy has done a great job fixing the Datsun. That new color he picked really pops. I can't wait to see how much he enjoys the new engine."

Phil starts to put the check in his pocket. "Thanks. Since you like what he has done with the car so much, I should have you guys talk. I think he might even be a better driver than me."

Mr. Daisuke smiles. "So that's why you wanted a similar setup on the Datsun as the GT-R. Well, my guys should be done with the Datsun next week. I will have them drop it off at your place as soon as I finish fine-tuning it and your new GT-R. That should give you a little time to drive it."

The plane comes to a stop, and Mr. Daisuke's flight attendant opens the door for Phil.

Phil looks at his watch. "I better get going. Brad's coming to pick me up. I think we are running a little bit late."

Mr. Daisuke nods. "We can finish this conversation at the party when I drop off the cars. I can't wait to get back to set up these races. I have a few hedge fund guys I can't wait to shut up."

Phil agrees. "That sounds like a plan. I can tell everybody then."

Phil and Mr. Daisuke tap their beer bottles together. They both take a drink and set the bottles on the table. Phil grabs his overnight bag and leaves the plane.

Brad is waiting in Phil's car. Phil walks out of the airport exit door. He gets in the passenger's side of the car with his bag.

He looks over at Brad in the driver's seat. "I really think you're going to enjoy your birthday present this year."

Brad starts the car and pulls away.

Brad looks over at Phil. "Does that have anything to do with why you extended your trip and why you had those guys picking up my car a couple of days ago?"

Phil tells him, "Maybe. Think that you and mom can handle running Phil's Pizza for a while?"

Brad laughs. "I knew it. You're going to get back into racing."

Brad fist-bumps Phil. They are both smiling.

Brad changes the subject. "I just hope you're over that argument with PJ. We're going to swing by his grand opening today, so you can meet all of Travis's old friends from his unit. Sometimes, dad, you just got to let things go and move on. He's really sorry about it."

—

Over at PJ's shop, PJ's looking out the front windows of his building at his contractors, who are putting up a new sign and taking away the old one that he destroyed with his Jeep. Doug, a current member of Tier One, comes in the back door and walks over to PJ.

Doug states, "So, Brad told me I missed one hell of a fight between you two. We're not going to have a repeat performance, are we?"

PJ tells him, "I'm sure Brad's going to bring him up to speed, and if he's anything like Travis, he's not going to show up if he doesn't want to be here."

Doug leaves and goes out back to the barbeque as PJ's satellite phone rings.

PJ picks up the phone. "Hello?"

On the other end of the line is Tiffany. She is at her CIA desk. She is watching a video that was filmed of Carlos detonating the IED that killed Travis and wounded PJ. Across from Tiffany is the little boy who filmed it and his mother, who appears to have been abused. There is an interpreter next to the mother instructing her on the paperwork and money placed before her.

The interpreter is explaining to the mother, "You understand that by signing this, you will be granted asylum to the United States. You and your son will be given new identities and a place to live. We will provide $500,000 cash and a job."

The mother takes the paperwork and signs it. She looks at the interpreter. "How soon can we leave?"

Tiffany is on the phone with PJ. "I've got some new intel, and we know what the fucker looks like now."

PJ is grateful. "Good to hear. If there's anything I can do, just let me know."

Tiffany explains, "I'm going to send you the intel as soon as I finish up here. Then you can share with your guys so when they get back, we can hit the ground running."

PJ says, "Thanks, I will. I know you guys will get the son of a bitch, and then you can come home too."

PJ hangs up the phone. He looks out the window and sees Brad pulling up. Brad turns into the parking lot as the contractor is pulling out of the parking lot. The contractor has finished putting up the new sign that says, "Tier One Tactical Shooting Range for all your Training Needs. RIP Matthew (2021), Mike (2019), AJ (2021), and Travis (2021): you will be missed until we regroup in Valhalla."

Brad parks the car, and PJ comes out the front door. Brad and Phil get out of the car and walk toward the front door. PJ greets Phil and Brad, and he extends his hand out for Phil to shake. PJ shakes Phil's hand.

PJ apologizes. "I'm sorry."

Phil accepts. "Don't worry about it, man. We all did stupid shit when we were young."

PJ laughs. "What do you mean young? I do stupid shit every day. Come on in. I want to introduce you to everybody."

Brad shakes PJ's hand. "I told you it would all work out."

PJ tells him, "I suppose you're going to want another free day at the range."

Brad smiles. "Okay, that'll work, but I think I'm going to outshoot you this time."

PJ laughs. "Oh, you're getting good, but not that good."

All three of them walk into the building.

Phil is impressed. "Wow, you really have a nice place, man."

The back wall is lined with guns, and display cases are full of guns. The storefront is almost completely set up.

PJ explains, "It's been slow going without Travis. This was mostly his baby. I wanted to do private security, but he and Tiffany talked me into doing this instead. I guess I should be thanking you for such a nice spot to build. Travis told me that you guys used to race here back in the day."

Phil looks at PJ. "It used to be one of his favorite spots to race on, and when it became available, I knew he would want it."

Brad pats his dad on the back. "I'm going to go grab some food. Why don't you two keep talking?"

Brad goes out the back door.

PJ tells Phil, "If you see anything you like, it's yours. It's the least I can do after I destroyed your car."

Phil waves PJ off. "No, I'm good. I have never had a need for a gun. I wouldn't even know how to use one."

PJ explains, "You know that's what I do here, right? I can show you everything you need to know."

Phil tells him, "I'll think about it. Why don't we head back and go grab some food? I'm kind of hungry."

They go to the back patio, where everybody else is sitting around the firepit having drinks and eating food. Jake is manning the grill. Robert is sitting next to Brian, who speaks up.

Brian calls out to Brad, "What took you so long?"

Brad tells him, "My dad's flight was late." Brad grabs a burger from the grill and sits down in one of the open chairs. "Okay, who's up next? I can't believe all the crazy shit you guys have done."

Brian is ready. "Okay, I got a good one for you. So, it's like 120 degrees, and we're like 200 yards away from anything that even resembles shade. PJ and I are lying down in some cover we made. We're waiting for some high-value targets to show up. Our drone operator informs us that the target is two mics out. We shoot out the tire of the SUV coming over the top of the hill. The SUV stops, and the men get out of the car to look at the tire. PJ and I take them out after we receive confirmation. Then these fuckers decide it'll be funny to pick us up in their vehicle. Conveniently enough, we seized eighty kilos of drugs from their vehicle. We got some great pics too."

Brad laughs. "I'm calling bullshit on that."

Brian smiles. "Oh, it's going to be like that."

Brian pulls out his phone and starts to show him some pictures. Phil and PJ come out of the back door laughing. Everybody starts to walk over to Phil and introduce themselves.

PJ motions for everyone to come over. "Hey, guys, this is Phil."

Phil goes around and shakes everyone's hands and introduces himself.

Brian shakes Phil's hand. "Brian."

Doug shakes Phil's hand. "Doug."

Robert shakes Phil's hand. "Robert."

Jake shakes Phil's hand. "Jake."

CHAPTER SEVENTEEN

The following evening, Phil is cleaning off a table as he yells out to Peggy, "Honey?…Honey!"

Peggy is dancing to music on her headset and singing along as she is finishing up mopping the floor. She lifts off her headset and looks up at Phil. "Yeah, baby?"

Phil looks down at his watch. "All we have left is to lock up. Do you want to go start the car, babe? We're running a little late."

Peggy tells him, "Okay, honey."

She places the headset back over her ears and puts the mop bucket in a closet, walks toward the back door, and exits. Phil finishes wiping down the tables, walks over to the "Open" sign, and shuts it off. As he is getting ready to lock the door, Carlos's two bodyguards come in through the front door.

Phil apologizes. "Sorry, guys, we're closing early. I have my son's party to get to. We will be open at eleven tomorrow."

Juan tells him, "We're not here for your crappy pizza."

Juan sucker punches Phil. Phil fights back. Phil is starting to gain the upper hand. Pedro pulls out his gun and shoots Phil in the ribs. Phil drops to one knee and covers the wound with one hand and braces himself against the wall with the other. Phil gets up and advances on them.

Pedro points to Phil. "Will you look at this shit?"

Juan turns to look, and Phil punches him, knocking him to the ground. Pedro shoots Phil again in the stomach.

Pedro laughs. "Fucker hits hard, doesn't he?"

Peggy appears at the back door. She notices Phil lying on the ground, hurt. She pulls off her headset. The two bodyguards are out of sight as Peggy makes her way over to Phil. She picks him up from off the ground.

Peggy asks him, "Baby, what happened?"

Phil whispers, "Run, baby, run." He passes out.

She is holding him as she starts to dial 911. As she hits the "Send" button, she looks up and sees the two bodyguards. Juan grabs the phone from Peggy and ends the call. Then he breaks the phone in half. Pedro shoots her in the chest.

Juan tells Pedro, "We need to torch this place."

They start scrambling around the pizza shop, finding things that are flammable and lighting them on fire. Pedro bends down and finds several small LP tanks in a small cabinet. They load several of the small LP tanks and throw them in the pizza oven. Pedro turns up the heat on the oven and heads outside and to the SUV. They drive off as the flames start to overtake the building.

—

Across town at PJ's shooting range, Brad and Josh are shooting some guns with PJ and the rest of his old unit behind them. Several of Phil and Brad's friends from the track are there as well for the upcoming party. Brad and Josh stop shooting once their guns are both empty and remove their ear plugs.

PJ calls out, "Everybody clear?"

Brad says, "Clear."

Josh says, "Clear."

PJ decides, "Well, I think Brad might have it."

Everybody starts to walk down the range to look at the targets.

Doug announces, "Well, whoever it is, this next round they're going down. Then I'm coming for you, big boy." He points at PJ.

Josh is walking side by side with Brad. "You have any idea why your dad had those guys pick up your car?"

Brad looks at Josh. "I think he said I cracked my block somehow."

Josh laughs. "Really, somehow? You don't think it was the second stage of nitrous or maybe you bumping the boost up?"

Brad mutters, "Yeah, yeah. I know."

Brad's phone starts to signal to him that there is a fire at the store. He looks at his phone and sees the message.

He turns to Josh. "You sure you got everything hooked up right on that new security system?"

Josh looks at Brad. "Of course, why?"

Brad panics. "There's a fire at the shop!"

Josh pulls out his cell phone and calls 911. Brad turns and starts running to Phil's car. He gets in the car and speeds away. At a two-way stop, the SUV comes to a stop. And in slow motion, Brad rounds the corner in front of them. The

SUV is being driven by Juan. Brad looks over as he passes the SUV and gets a good look at them.

Brad arrives in front of the pizza store. He slides into the parking lot in front of the building. The fire department, several police cars, and Captain Charles show up behind him. The fire department starts to put out the fire, and Captain Charles tries to move Brad back. All the people invited to the party start showing up.

Rachel comes up to Brad and comforts him. "Maybe they weren't inside, baby."

Josh gets Brad's attention about the app on his phone. "Let me see your phone, man."

Brad hands his phone to Josh. He starts looking through it to find the app for the security system and opens it. PJ comes up behind them. PJ is trying to call Phil's cell phone.

PJ looks over at Brad. "It's going straight to voice mail."

Josh is looking at Brad's phone. "Brad!"

Brad is in shock and does not acknowledge Josh talking to him.

Josh yells again, "Brad, you need to see this!"

Josh hands the phone back to Brad. Brad starts to watch the playback of the security cameras on his phone. PJ and Rachel are watching it also. Brad and Rachel start to tear up. PJ does not have a reaction. PJ looks over at his friends from his unit. They all give him a nod with their heads. PJ walks around in front of Brad. Brad, with tears coming down, looks at PJ with a very pissed-off look on his face.

PJ tells him, "I know that look. Hell, I had that same look on my face after I found out my parents were killed by a suicide bomber. Sometimes it takes good people doing bad things to make things right. You were there when I needed you. Let us be there for you now."

Brad looks over at the rest of PJ's unit. They all have serious looks on their faces as they nod to him.

Rachel tells him, "Your dad has lots of friends in the police department. They can handle this."

Captain Charles waves Brad over. "Your mom made a 911 call, but then the phone cut out. Do you have any idea what was going on here?"

Brad slides his phone back into his pocket. "No."

Captain Charles tells him, "Hopefully I can get some answers for you soon. Why don't you go ahead and head home? I'll come by later if I have something for you. There's nothing you can do here now."

Brad is still in shock. "Okay, thank you."

Brad turns around and walks back over to Rachel, PJ, and Josh.

Rachel asks him, "You told him what happened, right?"

Brad is getting upset. "No, I'm going to handle this."

Rachel begs him, "No, you need to let the cops do their job."

Brad informs her, "If you love me, please, just let me do this."

Brad turns and looks at Josh. Amanda, Josh's girlfriend, is standing next to Josh.

Brad asks Josh, "Can you take the girls home? Then meet us back at my place."

Josh tells him, "Yeah, no problem."

Rachel turns to Josh. "You're going to talk some sense into him, right?"

Josh explains, "I'll try, but first let's get you home."

Firemen are fighting the fire that has completely engulfed the store while Brad, PJ, and his unit stand by the cars. Josh, Rachel, and Amanda get in the car and drive away.

CHAPTER EIGHTEEN

Brad, Josh, PJ, and the rest of Tier One are gathered at Brad's house. They are sitting around the kitchen table. PJ is on his satellite phone and talking to Colonel Hightower.

PJ is asking him, "Do you still want me to train the new guys? Or do you want to keep looking for Travis's and my replacements in that stack of papers on your desk?"

PJ assumes Colonel Hightower must be sitting at his desk with a huge pile of papers in front of him.

Colonel Hightower tells him, "I'm glad you finally realized retirement's not for you."

PJ tries to bargain with the colonel. "I'll do it for the same price that Travis was going to charge. And I'm going to need the box for a week."

Colonel Hightower states, "You know I can't deploy the box on U.S. soil."

PJ finishes up, "Well, that's my price; take it or leave it."

A big custom semi rig pulls up out in front of the house. On the side of the trailer, it says, "Daisuke Auto." Mr. Daisuke comes out of the passenger's side as the men in the semitrailer start to unload Brad's Datsun and Phil's GT-R.

Mr. Daisuke walks up to the front door and knocks on it. Brad opens the door.

Mr. Daisuke looks at Brad. "Brad? Man, you have grown so much. So, where is your dad? He hasn't been answering his phone all morning."

Brad starts to tear up. "My dad was robbed last night, and they killed him and my mom."

Mr. Daisuke looks confused. "What?"

Brad tries to explain. "He fought back."

Mr. Daisuke is crushed. "I'm so sorry for your loss. Is there anything I can do for you?"

Behind Mr. Daisuke, Brad's Datsun is being unloaded from the semitrailer.

Brad looks over at the semi. "Is that my car?"

Mr. Daisuke is still processing the information. "Yes, but we can get to that later. We need to talk."

Brad explains, "All my dad said is our lives were going to change a little bit because he was going to get back into racing with you."

Josh and the rest of PJ's unit start to head out the front door, passing Brad's car. Brad and PJ stay behind on the front porch. Josh stops and looks at Brad's car as the hood is being opened. The rest of the unit goes on to PJ's Jeep.

Josh calls out to Brad, "Looks like you're going to get one hell of a last present from your dad."

Brad tells him, "Yeah, he said I was going to really love my present. I suppose I have you to thank for that." He looks over at Mr. Daisuke.

Mr. Daisuke tells him, "Your dad only wanted the best for you. You don't think they knew about the money that I paid him for his buyout, do you?"

Brad asks him, "So you think they killed him over a little bit of money?"

Mr. Daisuke says, "Well, I wouldn't say a little bit of money. That kind of money tends to get you noticed."

Brad tells him, "If I didn't know about it yet, I'm sure they didn't know. My dad was so excited to start driving for you again. He told me if I ever got the opportunity to drive one of your new builds, I would never look at my car the same way."

Mr. Daisuke smiles. "I appreciate that, but my cars are only as good as the driver behind the wheel. Your dad was the best driver I have ever known. Now, if you can excuse me, I need to make a few phone calls and push this race back until I can find a driver who will push my cars as hard as your dad did."

Mr. Daisuke starts to make a phone call as he walks across the front yard to the semitrailer and his race team.

PJ looks over at Brad. "Once we get our gear, it should only take a few days to get these guys."

Brad is grateful. "I appreciate you doing this for me. I wouldn't be able to do this alone."

PJ explains, "You were there when I needed you. I will always be there if you need anything. We also have your video; that's going to be a big help in tracking these guys down quickly."

Josh comes over to Brad and PJ. The rest of Tier One are still waiting for Josh by PJ's Jeep.

Brad asks Josh, "How's it look, man?"

Josh smiles. "You're not going to believe this. They swapped out your engine, man."

Brad walks over to the car. The hood is open. The men who were unloading the cars are standing next to it. They hand Brad the keys as Brad reaches the car. Brad and Josh are both looking at the engine. It is a RB26 with a big turbo. Brad starts to cry. PJ and Mr. Daisuke come over to the car. The rest of Tier One start gathering around Brad, Josh, and the car.

Mr. Daisuke looks over at Brad. "Your dad had me make some serious upgrades. He thought you would appreciate it."

Brad asks him, "Do you know who you are going to get to replace my dad?"

Mr. Daisuke laughs. "I've been trying to replace your dad forever. It's not an easy task."

Brad looks at him seriously. "Did my dad ever talk about me possibly driving for you?"

Mr. Daisuke tells him, "He mentioned it, but the GT-R is set up for your dad. If you drive anything like him, it'd be my honor to have you behind the wheel of my car. Are you sure you feel up to it so soon?"

Brad looks at Mr. Daisuke. "I really don't know. I'm just trying to figure out what I'm going to do next. I always loved driving, and my dad always told me if you can do something that you love, you're not really working."

Rachel pulls up in her car. She gets out and walks over to Brad.

Rachel tells him, "My parents said we could use their cabin if you want to get out of the house."

Brad tells her, "That sounds nice, but we just need a few days to figure things out here."

Rachel embraces Brad. "I don't agree with you doing this, but I'll have your back no matter what you want to do."

Brad suggests, "Why don't you go back to your place, and I'll stop by later? Maybe we can go out of town in a few days."

Rachel asks him, "Where do you want to go?"

Brad shrugs. "I don't know."

Brad walks Rachel to her car and opens her door for her.

Rachel gives him a kiss. "Don't be too long, baby. You know I'm here for you. I just wanted to check on you. I've got some stuff I want to take care of at home anyways."

Rachel drives away. Tier One and Josh take off in PJ's Jeep back to the gun shop. PJ and Mr. Daisuke walk up behind Brad. Brad looks over at Mr. Daisuke.

Mr. Daisuke tells him, "If there is anything I can ever do for you, just let me know."

Brad looks over at his dad's car. "Wouldn't mind the opportunity to take that GT-R for a spin."

Mr. Daisuke looks over to the men who unloaded the Datsun and the GT-R. Mr. Daisuke motions over to Lee. Lee comes over and hands the keys to the GT-R to Mr. Daisuke. Mr. Daisuke, in turn, turns to Brad and hands him the keys.

Mr. Daisuke tells him, "It would be a complete shame to load that beautiful piece of machinery back up on the trailer without it being driven. Please let me know what you think and if she's track-ready or if I need to make any adjustments. And take Lee with you in case you have any questions."

Brad says, "Thank you."

Brad and Lee walk over and get into the highly modified GT-R. They put on their seat belts, back out of the driveway, and do a nice holeshot down the street. Brad is tearing up the streets, pushing the car to its limits. He takes a few corners and progressively gets faster and faster.

Lee informs him, "You can't do this on these streets. You're going too fast."

Brad has a huge smile on his face. Lee is getting scared of how hard Brad is pushing the car on the streets.

—

Back at Brad's house, PJ and Mr. Daisuke are on the porch talking.

Mr. Daisuke sighs. "I still can't believe they killed my friend. All of this over some money."

PJ shakes his head. "I'm not sure it was all over money, but I do know they are not going to get away with it. I've spent a lifetime tracking down worse people than this."

Brad comes down the street in the GT-R. He pulls into the driveway and shuts off the car. Lee gets out and starts to yell at Mr. Daisuke.

Lee yells, "This fucking guy is crazy!"

Mr. Daisuke informs him, "Yeah, he really is a chip off the old block."

Lee walks over to talk to Mr. Daisuke and PJ. Mr. Daisuke motions to Lee's pants. They notice that he has pissed himself. Mr. Daisuke and PJ chuckle. Brad walks away from the GT-R. Lee turns and walks toward the semitrailer.

Lee is muttering to himself in Japanese, "Fucking asshole."

Brad laughs. "Yeah, my dad was right. I'll never look at my Datsun the same way. Thank you."

Mr. Daisuke tells him, "I am going to head to the hotel. If you need anything, just call. I have to get these guys on the road to Vegas."

Mr. Daisuke pulls out a stack of business cards and hands one of them to Brad. Mr. Daisuke's team loads the GT-R back up and heads to the hotel.

Brad looks over at PJ. "When do we start?"

PJ tells him, "Let's go to my place."

Brad and PJ get into Brad's Datsun and head to PJ's gun shop.

CHAPTER NINETEEN

The next day PJ is in front of the building just getting out of his Jeep. He is on the satellite phone with Colonel Hightower.

PJ tells him, "Thanks for helping us get our gear. We should have things wrapped up here in about a week."

Colonel Hightower informs him, "They should be swinging by any minute now. And I'll start sending recruits your way soon."

PJ is grateful. "I look forward to meeting them. I will talk to you soon."

PJ looks up as he hears the helicopter. The helicopter stops over the back of the shooting range and drops a big military shipping crate. Tiffany propels down to the ground from the helicopter. She gives the helicopter the okay to leave with a hand signal.

The helicopter releases the cables and flies off. The cables drop around the crate. Everybody from Tier One but PJ goes over and meets Tiffany at the crate. Brad is left at the shooting table. Tiffany jumps down off the crate and starts to greet everyone. She removes her helmet.

Tiffany calls out, "What have you got yourselves into, boys? Figured I'd take a break to help you out."

Brad is shooting a rifle at a target about three hundred yards away. There's a small pile of paper targets sitting next to him on the table. They all have the bullseye shot out of them. Brad is changing out his mags on the rifle he is shooting and starts to shoot again. PJ comes out the back door of the shooting range and walks up behind everybody.

PJ looks over at Doug. "How long has he been here?"

Doug tells him, "He showed up just after you left."

PJ takes a drink out of his coffee. After he sets the coffee down, he picks up the stack of targets Brad has been shooting at. PJ starts to thumb through them and sees that he hasn't missed. The ten spot is shot out of them. PJ sets the targets back down.

PJ calls over to Brad, "Brad. Cease-fire."

Brad looks at PJ as he walks over to him. PJ looks at Doug. Doug grabs duct tape and a two-by-four off one of the shooting benches. He hands them over to PJ. PJ pulls a quarter out of his pocket.

Brad asks, "What's with the crate?"

PJ tells him, "I called in a favor."

PJ tapes a quarter onto the piece of wood. PJ turns and heads downrange. Doug waves over the rest of Tier One as they're all sitting around the firepit. Everyone from Tier One, except for Brian, who is talking with Tiffany, walks over to Brad, who is sitting at a shooting table. They all gather around and proceed to take off their necklaces and put them on the shooting table in front of Brad. They have a quarter with a hole shot out of them.

Doug explains, "There are two things you need to do become a part of Tier One. Save a member's life, and make this shot when called upon. You have already proved yourself by being there for PJ. So just make the shot."

Brad looks downrange at the target. PJ is standing next to it.

Brad is nervous. "He's coming back, right?"

Doug laughs. "No. It's going to be his life on the line downrange when we do this. He wants to know that you can make the shot."

Brad looks down at the table where all the necklaces are. Doug pulls out his sidearm and starts shooting at a different steel target. Brad looks over at Doug. Doug sees Brad looking over.

Doug starts laughing. "What? You think it's going to be all nice and quiet when the bullets start flying? Just make the shot, buttercup."

As Brad grabs the rifle, everything slows down. Brad looks down the rifle scope. Doug is still shooting in the background. Brad takes a deep breath and lines up his shot; you can hear his heart beating. Brad squeezes the trigger slowly. He strikes the target, putting a hole directly through the middle of the quarter with PJ standing next to it. Brad stops shooting, and the rest of Tier One start to pick up their necklaces.

Brian and Tiffany stop talking as PJ is walking back from the target. Tiffany walks over to Brad and extends her hand out for him to shake.

Tiffany tells him, "Thank you."

Brad is a little confused. "What for?"

Tiffany explains, "Thanks for being there for PJ."

Brad tells her, "I just did what any of you would have done."

Tiffany walks back over to Brian. PJ comes over to Brad and shakes his hand. He gives Brad the quarter he shot. "Good shooting. Now let's get to work."

CHAPTER TWENTY

Brad arrives at Rachel's house the following morning. He parks his car and walks up to the front door. Before he gets a chance to knock, the door opens. Rachel's mother, Marilyn, is standing there.

Marilyn's arms are outstretched. "Get over here."

As she hugs Brad, Rachel's father, John, comes around the corner.

Brad looks at both of them. "Can I talk to you guys?"

John smiles. "Yes, of course. Rachel should be down in just a moment. Do you have any idea what you're going to do now?"

Brad tells him, "I was thinking about rebuilding my dad's business, but it's just going to take some time. Or possibly do some racing for my dad's old partner."

John encourages Brad. "I'm sure you will figure things out. Maybe Rachel can help you. She's been working on arrangements for your parents this morning."

Brad is grateful. "I appreciate that, but that's not what I wanted to talk to you about. John and Marilyn, I'd like to ask you both if I can have your daughter's hand in marriage.

She completes me, and with everything that's going on, I don't want to wait any longer."

Marilyn and John both are happy and give their blessing.

John shakes Brad's hand. "Yes, of course."

Marilyn hugs Brad. "Yes."

Rachel enters the room. "I tried to make some funeral arrangements for your parents, but I couldn't get any information. They're going to need to talk to you since I'm not next of kin."

Brad looks over at Rachel's parents. "See? This is why I love this woman so much."

Brad turns back to Rachel. He gets down on one knee and pulls out the ring he's been carrying around for years from his pocket.

Brad starts, "Rachel Mary Catherine Whitmore, will you…?"

Rachel does not let him finish his proposal. "Yes!"

———

Back at the gun range with everybody from Tier One, Josh is sleeping in a chair next to Doug. Doug is operating a drone from a small desk with a laptop and joystick sitting on top of it. Brian is making some small explosive devices. Everybody else is cleaning guns and loading magazines with ammunition.

Doug motions everyone over. "Hey guys, I think I might have found them."

PJ sighs. "I really hope this is the right one. I really don't need to see any more soccer moms."

Doug laughs. "Really? That last one was fucking hot, and you know it. You do realize how many black SUVs there are in Iowa? Brian, can you take over for me? I need some rack time."

PJ looks over at Josh. "Josh, you want to call Brad? Just tell him we could use his help at the range."

—

Across town Brad and Rachel are celebrating their engagement. They are holding hands across the table. Brad's phone rings.

Brad is a little anxious. "Hey, please tell me you guys have some good news."

Josh informs him, "You should probably make your way back here."

Brad tells him, "Okay, I'll be there soon as I can. I just have to drop off Rachel."

Brad motions to the waiter for the check. Rachel overhears the conversation on the phone. When Brad hangs up, she tries to reason with him.

Rachel reminds him, "You know it's not too late to let the police handle this."

Brad tells her, "We talked about this, babe. There's no way I could live with myself knowing that these people did this to my parents and I stood by and did nothing."

The waiter comes back with the check.

—

Back at the shooting range, Brian stops loading ammo into magazines. He comes over to the desk to relieve Doug. He takes over the controls of the drone. Doug goes and lays down on a makeshift bed that is sitting in the corner behind the desk.

Brian tells him, "Thirty-two hours straight. That might be a new record for you."

Doug raises his hand in the background and gives a thumbs-up.

Brian wonders out loud, "Is that…?"

PJ walks over to Brian and looks over his shoulder. The camera from the drone pans down from high above John's car lot. They find the black SUV parked beside the semi-trailer transport. The two bodyguards are nearby. Carlos and Chris are instructing them to load a couple of vehicles on a big semitrailer transport. The drone zooms in closer on Carlos and Chris, sending their pictures back to PJ's shop.

PJ is in shock. "Are you fucking kidding me?"

Tiffany is angry. "I have my whole team looking for him in Afghanistan, and he's here?"

PJ goes over to a small safe in the box and pulls out a file labeled "Tier One Eyes Only." He brings it over to Tiffany. They open it up to find pictures and documentation of Carlos. There is one photo of Carlos's father, Gabriel.

Brian tells them, "I can't get a positive ID; we're going to have to get it some other way."

PJ reluctantly states, "I'm going to need to bring the cops in on this. We're not dealing with street thugs."

Brad shows up at PJ's gun range, and Josh meets him in the front of the shop.

Josh is concerned. "So, are you really going to do this?"

Brad explains, "My parents never deserved to die like that. Wouldn't you?"

Josh nods in agreement with Brad.

Brad goes on, "My dad was a very forgiving man. And I like to think my dad passed that quality onto me. But killing my parents? No way in hell I'm going to let that shit go."

Brad and Josh head back to the crate.

PJ is giving final instructions. "Brian, I want you in the back of the truck with Brad. Robert, I want you in the box providing overwatch with Josh."

Doug is excited. "Let's see how they like losing a shipment."

PJ continues, "I don't want any surprises on this one. Tiffany and Jake, you've got the body shop. Doug, you'll be my secondary shooter after you put in the explosives. We'll have a little chat with them tomorrow. I better go bring the cops up to speed on this. I'm sure they don't have the resources to deal with somebody like him. I don't like turning my new home into a war zone, but we need to put an end to this."

CHAPTER TWENTY-ONE

A couple days later, PJ pulls into the dealership as it is closing. Juan and Pedro are loading up several vehicles onto a semitrailer.

Carlos tells them, "Load up the black one first. Then the red one, followed by the silver. Then my SUV."

Below the paint shop, Tiffany and Jake are armed and ready to breach a door.

Tiffany whispers, "Are we clear?"

Back at the shooting range, Josh is sitting with his laptop in the shipping crate. He disables the security system feed to the area below the paint shop.

Josh tells them, "Both my security and their secondary security are down. You're clear to go."

Tiffany picks the lock. Jake opens the door and throws two flash-bangs into the room. After the flash-bangs go off, Tiffany is the first through the door. Two drug dealer workers are struggling to draw their weapons. Tiffany disarms and knocks out the first worker. Jake knocks out the second one. After subduing the workers, Tiffany and Jake finish clearing the room.

Jake says, "Clear."

Tiffany says, "Clear." She radios above, "Drug lab secure with two detained."

~

Before the black SUV is loaded from inside the body shop, Juan presses an intercom button by some toolboxes on the wall.

Juan tells the crew down below, "Boss says three more carloads next week."

PJ is sitting in his Jeep. He hears Tiffany's "drug lab secure" and gets out.

Carlos looks over at Chris. "You told me he wasn't going to be an issue."

He motions over to PJ as he is getting out of his Jeep. Juan and Pedro finish loading the last of the vehicles onto the semitrailer and start to walk over to Carlos and Chris. Chris turns to see PJ. Carlos walks over with Chris to talk to PJ.

PJ starts to speak as they walk over. "I don't really care who your new friends are, but it needs to end now."

Chris tells him, "Who I do business with is none of your fucking business."

PJ sarcastically slow-claps his hands together. "A drug dealer and murderers, well done. The way I see it, there are two types of currency in life. The type I have earned and the type you have. You need to give five million compensation to Brad or you're going to see what the type of currency I have earned can buy."

At that moment Juan pulls out a handgun and points it at PJ.

PJ tells him, "Why don't you put that down before you hurt yourself?"

Carlos motions to Juan to put the gun down. Juan lowers his gun.

Carlos looks over at Chris. "He's giving you a way out here. He's not going to the police. Just go ahead and pay the man."

Juan is upset. "You're going to give this asshole a free pass after he ratted you out? Now you are going to let him do this?" He raises his gun back up to PJ. "It was only one man and his crappy pizza shop."

PJ looks surprised. "Crappy? Are you fucking kidding me? Phil made the best pizza you ever had."

Chris looks at Juan and Pedro. "What did you do? You were only supposed to rough him up."

Juan explains, "He got out of hand. We had to put him down."

Chris is furious. "Are you fucking kidding me? Put him down? I didn't want him killed."

PJ looks at Juan. "Put your gun down. I won't be telling you again."

Juan looks at Carlos. "Let me put an end to this so we can get on the road."

Carlos looks over to Chris. He motions for Juan to put his gun down, and Juan obeys.

Carlos tells Chris, "Look, man, we got a good thing going here. Let's not fuck it up. Just pay the man and move past it."

Juan shakes his head. "No, no, fuck that man. I'll do him right here."

PJ points to Juan. "Why don't you just let the adults talk here?"

Juan starts moving closer to PJ while raising the gun up to PJ's face a third time. PJ disarms him and knocks him to the ground. PJ disassembles the gun and throws the pieces back at him. Juan picks up the pieces that were dropped and starts to reassemble the gun. He stands back up and starts to raise it at PJ again.

Brian and Brad are lying down in the back of an old pickup truck. They are looking through rifle scopes with the tailgate down about three hundred yards away from the car lot.

Brian says, "Send it."

Brad squeezes the trigger, sending the shot down the street directly into Juan's chest.

PJ looks over to Chris as Juan falls to the ground from being shot by Brad.

PJ calmly looks at Chris. "So, what's it going to be, Chris?"

Chris is surprised. "Whoa! What the fuck?"

Pedro leans down and checks for a pulse. He stands and draws his handgun from his back and starts to raise it toward PJ.

Carlos and Chris both yell at Pedro, "No!"

Brad, looking through his rifle scope, squeezes the trigger a second time, shooting Pedro through the chest.

PJ explains, "At least they had a chance. Phil was unarmed and outnumbered. Why would you have idiots like that working for you? War is hell, but I suppose it's good for business for you. But since you're involved with those guys, the price just tripled. Chris, this debt is on you."

PJ starts to turn and walk to his Jeep. Carlos and Chris are standing there speechless as PJ stops and turns back around.

PJ tells them, "It probably goes without saying, but from the looks of your help, you guys aren't very bright. I wouldn't move for a while, and enjoy the fireworks. I know I will."

PJ starts to walk to his Jeep again.

Carlos calls out, "Hey, what do you mean fireworks?"

PJ laughs as he walks away. He explains, "Bring it by the strip club off Sixth Street at midnight tomorrow. I'll get the money to Brad. Consider it your life insurance."

Carlos says, "So, I guess this is the cost of doing business, then. He pays you, and we can walk away."

PJ promises, "I'll give you my word. Not one man from my unit or Brad will harm Chris. By the way, you guys got that, right?" PJ points to Juan and Pedro.

At that moment, small explosions start to happen among all the high-end sports cars that were just loaded onto the semitrailer, except for the black SUV. Carlos and Chris both jump away from the explosions.

PJ gets in his Jeep and drives away.

Carlos and Chris start to argue.

Chris is upset. "Goddamn it. I told them just to kick his ass."

Carlos holds his hands up. "Hey, don't look at me. You're the one who started this whole thing. You asked for their help. What did you think was going to happen?"

Carlos pushes Chris. Carlos pulls out his phone and texts his father: "We might have a problem."

Near the exit Doug stands up from behind a car on the car lot. He puts the trigger for the bombs back in his pocket. He picks up his rifle and two black bags and walks down the road a bit before PJ pulls up in his Jeep and they drive away.

CHAPTER TWENTY-TWO

Everyone has gathered for Phil and Peggy's memorial. Mr. Daisuke is talking to one of Phil's friends in the background. Brad is sitting on the couch with Rachel next to him. They both have plates of food in front of them.

Brad is grateful. "I really appreciate everything you did, babe. It was a great service."

Rachel tells him, "You know I would do anything for you."

Rachel sets down her plate of food and comforts him. PJ and Josh walk over to Brad. Rachel picks up her plate of food.

PJ tells him, "When you get a minute, we need to talk. I think Josh has a pretty good idea."

Brad stands up and sets his plate of food on the coffee table, and all three of them start to walk toward the back bedroom. Brad, PJ, and Josh gather to talk. PJ has his plate of food with him to eat while they are talking.

Josh looks at Brad. "What would you think if we gave him back his drugs?"

Brad is confused. "Why in the hell would we want to do that?"

Josh explains, "Revenge is a dish best served cold, right? With that amount of drugs, he will never get out of jail. Especially since you are going to take his bankroll."

Brad asks him, "How in the hell are we going to give him his drugs back?"

Josh tells him, "I got you, man. That dealership was one of my first clients. I should probably stop by and do a security check. I think they were having issues last night. I am pretty sure they need a new hard drive." Josh laughs.

As they are leaving the bedroom, PJ pulls Brad aside. "Is there anything you can do to relax? I need you with a clear head tonight."

Rachel comes up to Brad in the hallway. "Honey, have you thought about what you want to do with your parents' ashes?"

Brad looks in the doorway of his parents' bedroom and sees his mom's purple fingernail polish bottle sitting alone on the nightstand. He walks into the bedroom and picks it up and puts it in his pocket. He goes into the living room and walks up to Brandon.

Brad asks, "Hey, would it be okay if I use your paint booth in a little bit?"

Brandon smiles. "Sure, what are we painting now? Your car looks great."

Later that day Brad is at a workbench preparing the paint gun with his parents' urns next to him. He sprinkles a bit of their ashes into the paint gun and mixes the paint. The paint color matches his mom's new favorite fingernail polish.

—

Meanwhile Josh heads to the car lot. He pulls out his phone and starts looking through the cameras. He sees there is no one there and pulls into the car lot. Beside him are two duffel bags. He has two black rubber gloves on. As he gets out of the car, he grabs the two duffel bags. He pulls out his phone and unlocks the door with his phone. He walks to the security office. On the door there is a sign that reads, "Security Personnel Only." Josh unlocks the door with his phone.

Josh sits down at the desk with the monitors. He pauses the camera feed. He goes to Chris's office and plants the drugs. Josh puts one of the duffel bags under the couch in Chris's office. He then places some drugs in Chris's desk. The remaining drugs he takes to the showroom and plants in one of the showroom cars.

Josh returns to the security office and deletes all the files and videos. He pulls the hard drive from the security system and replaces it with another. He sets it up to start recording in thirty minutes. Then Josh, with the original hard drive in his hand, leaves the building and gets into his car. He exits the car lot.

—

A few blocks away, Chris is sitting in his home office drinking a scotch. On his desk are three black duffel bags. Tom walks in with a packed bag.

Tom tells him, "I don't know why you are insisting on sending me to mom's house."

Chris explains, "I should have told you this sooner, but I have been shipping drugs out of the dealership for a while now. It looks like it's coming back to bite me in the ass. I just want to make sure you are out of harm's way. Hopefully after tonight, everything will be okay."

Chris sees on his computer monitor that Carlos and his two new bodyguards have shown up. Chris turns to Tom. "Why don't you head on out the back door?"

Tom turns to leave. Chris invites Carlos and his two bodyguards in. They head to his home office.

Chris starts, "I'm not sure this is a good idea. How do you know there won't be some retaliation?"

Carlos waves him off. "Stop stressing out. They're after your money, not your life. We can make that back in six months. I had to get a couple PMCs until I can get some of my guys across the border. We will not have any issues with these guys. They come highly recommended."

Carlos puts a small IED shaped like a money stack into one of the bags.

Carlos tells him, "But if things aren't going the way we want, I'll have a little surprise for them.

CHAPTER TWENTY-THREE

PJ, Brad, and the rest of the unit are sitting in the strip club with women all around them. Tiffany is in the background, dancing on stage. Chris and Carlos, with his two bodyguards, enter the strip club. PJ recognizes the two new bodyguards as Greg and Danny from previous military training.

PJ welcomes the group. "Nice of you gentlemen to finally show up. We were almost out of money."

Chris and the two bodyguards drop the three duffel bags in front of PJ and Brad.

Carlos looks at PJ. "We're good now, right?"

PJ looks over at Brad and gives everyone a nod. PJ leans over and unzips one of the bags and opens it up to reveal the money. Rex, with a service dog vest on, signals to PJ that one of the bags has something in it.

PJ notices. "Now that the business is out of the way, why don't we have some fun, boys?"

PJ waves Tiffany over. He reaches down and pulls out a small stack of money and hands it to Tiffany.

PJ tells her, "Why don't you give my new friend here that private dance that you were talking about earlier?"

Tiffany grabs Carlos by the hand and starts to lead him to the VIP room. The bodyguards start to follow him.

Carlos stops them. "Why don't you stay out here and keep our new friends company? See, Chris? It's just business."

Tiffany asks Carlos, "Are you ready to have the time of your life?"

Carlos smiles. "Always. You must be new here."

Tiffany tells him, "Yeah, it's my first time here. Enough about me. Let's go have some fun."

Back where PJ, Chris, and the rest of the crew are sitting, Greg speaks up. "Master Chief, good to see you again."

Danny tells him, "We're sorry to hear about Travis."

PJ tells both of them, "We're about ready to fix that problem. Your new boss was the trigger man who set off the IED that killed Travis. Why don't you grab that bag right there and enjoy retirement, boys? We'll handle it."

Greg starts to apologize. "If we had known, Master Chief, we would have never taken the job."

Danny noticed that Rex called out the bag with the bomb in it. "I see Rex hasn't lost his touch."

Greg bends down, pets Rex on the head, and picks up one of the bags. They both nod at PJ and everybody from his unit. They proceed to walk out the door with the bag in hand.

Chris is worried. "Oh, fuck, please, man, you don't have to do this. I didn't mean for Phil to get killed."

PJ tells him, "We did have a deal. You lived up to your end of the bargain. Your partner, on the other hand? He never had a deal. I don't deal with terrorists. That motherfucker cost me my leg and my best friend."

Brad stands up and tells Chris, "I know you probably didn't intend on having my dad killed, but you took everything from me. Why don't you go home and let that sink in?"

Chris apologizes. "I'm sorry. You know I never intended for things to go so far."

Chris stands up and leaves the strip club.

PJ waves over the owner and bouncer, Ed. PJ picks up the bag without the bomb and hands it to Brad. Brad hands it over to Ed.

Brad is grateful. "Thanks for your understanding, and this should cover any damages. Just make sure we get that hard drive for the security system."

Ed tells him, "Not a problem, man. Anything for your dad. I'm sure going to miss his pizzas, though."

PJ starts heading to the VIP room. As he is walking in, Tiffany is taking a sexy selfie with Carlos to get verification. PJ comes into the room.

Carlos is looking over at PJ. "What's up?"

PJ pulls out his gun and points it at Carlos. Carlos looks at the gun.

Carlos is shocked. "What the fuck?"

Tiffany sends off the picture to the CIA and sets her phone on the table in front of them.

～

Tiffany's selfie comes into the war room. The receiving officer runs it through facial recognition and starts comparing it with other intelligence that has been received and the video shot by the Taliban's little boy. It is a match.

—

The phone on the table starts to buzz in a signal that it is a positive match. Carlos starts to stand up. PJ shoots him in the left kneecap.

PJ tells him, "That's for me, you piece of shit. Sit down."

Carlos yells, "Greg, Danny, get in here!"

Carlos falls back into the chair and sits down.

Tiffany laughs. "You think money makes somebody loyal to you? Try spending five years in the shit having their back every day. Then you might have a clue what true loyalty is. You hired two of the most highly decorated Tier One members there are. Well, that is, excluding my husband and PJ."

Carlos grabs his leg in pain. Tiffany starts putting on her blue jeans and a tank top. She slips on a pair of brass knuckles. PJ hands Tiffany a small IED shaped like a stack of money.

Tiffany smiles and sarcastically says, "Oh, isn't that nice? You brought me a present. Hopefully you enjoy the one I brought you."

Tiffany turns and shows Carlos the IED.

Carlos looks at PJ. "I thought we had a deal."

PJ explains, "No, Chris had the deal; you had nothing, you piece of shit. You killed my friend, and I don't make deals with terrorists."

PJ still has his gun pointed at Carlos as Tiffany walks over to Carlos and drops the IED into his lap. She starts punching Carlos in the face and breaks his nose. She starts to search him. Tiffany finds two phones on Carlos's person.

She opens them up and finds that one only has one number saved in its call history.

Tiffany tells him, "You really shouldn't have killed my husband." Tiffany turns and walks out of the VIP room.

Carlos turns to PJ. "How much is this going to cost me? Everybody has their price."

PJ looks him right in the eye. "I want my friend back. Can you really buy that?"

Carlos starts to beg. "Just don't…"

PJ puts two shots into Carlos's chest and one in his head, killing him. PJ leaves the VIP room.

Everybody except for PJ and Tiffany is already outside of the strip club. Josh is pulling into the parking lot in his car. He parks next to all the people. PJ and Tiffany are coming out the front door. Ed walks over to Josh and hands him a hard drive. Josh pulls out a black light pen and looks at the hard drive that states "Fuessley Security Systems" in special ink. Josh looks up and sees Tiffany. He gives her a thumbs-up. Doug is standing next to one of the strippers, who is calling 911 and reading a prewritten text off Doug's phone.

The 911 operator picks up. "911. What's your emergency?"

The stripper is nervous but begins reading the text off the phone. "I need the police to come to the Ranch. There's a guy threatening to blow up the place. We're all outside, and he's still in there."

The 911 operator tells her, "I have police en route."

The stripper hangs up her phone. Doug hands her some cash, and he deletes the text on his phone. Across the parking lot, Tiffany hits "Send" on the phone. It detonates the bomb, blowing up most of the strip club. Josh walks over to Brad.

Josh smiles. "Can we throw one hell of a party or what?"

Brad laughs as he pulls out his phone, and he texts Mr. Daisuke: "If you're still willing to give me a shot behind the wheel of your race car, I can catch a flight tonight and be ready to race for you tomorrow."

CHAPTER TWENTY-FOUR

Brad and Rachel wake up the next morning looking at each other. Their hands touch, showing the new wedding bands on their fingers. Brad gets up out of bed. Brad, still in his underwear, heads to the bathroom to brush his teeth. Brad's phone pings in a signal for an incoming text.

Rachel calls out, "You want me to get that, baby?"

Brad tells her, "Sure."

Rachel checks the phone. Rachel gets out bed, still in her underwear as well, walks over to Brad, and hugs him from behind.

Rachel tells him, "They want us at the track by ten."

Brad finishes brushing his teeth and turns around. He gives Rachel a big hug.

Brad has a smirk on his face. "So, what you're saying is we have a couple hours?"

Brad kisses Rachel and then picks her up. He carries her back to the bed.

CHAPTER TWENTY-FIVE

Later that day, inside Mr. Daisuke's race trailer that is being pulled by a semi sit Mr. Daisuke, PJ, and Lee. They are all sitting and relaxing while having a few drinks and watching TV. There comes across the TV a breaking news flash.

The newscaster reports, "There has been a suspected terrorist attack at a gentleman's club. More to come, as investigations are still ongoing. We also have reports of police, FBI, and DEA presence at a car dealership for suspected drug trafficking."

Across the intercom, the driver radios, "Mr. Daisuke, Brad's signaling to pull over. What would you like me to do, sir?"

Mr. Daisuke says, "Pull over. See what's going on."

Brad is pulling off the road in his freshly painted Datsun with Rachel asleep in the passenger's seat. It is the same deep purple as his mom's fingernail polish. On top of the car, it states in white lettering, "In Loving Memory of." The driver's side lists "Phil," and the passenger's side lists "Peggy." The road overlooks the ocean, and Mr. Daisuke's race team is behind him. Rachel starts to wake up as Brad pulls the car over. She lifts the sunglasses that are covering her eyes.

Rachel looks at Brad lovingly. "Are we there?"

Brad tells her, "Almost, baby. I just need to make a stop to send my dad a message."

Rachel grabs Brad's hand and kisses it. He reaches into the cupholder and grabs the empty glass juice bottle. It has a small piece of paper in it. Brad and Rachel get out of the car and walk over to the edge of the cliff overlooking the ocean.

PJ and Mr. Daisuke come out of the side door of the semitrailer. They start to walk over to Brad and Rachel as Brad throws the bottle into the ocean.

PJ looks at Brad. "What's going on?"

Brad tells him, "Just letting my parents know we are going to be okay."

PJ puts his arm around Brad's neck. He starts to pour out most of his beer onto the ground. "To the road less traveled, and the friends and family who travel it with us."

There is a sunrise on a beach in heaven. The bottle that Brad threw into the ocean has washed up on the shore. Phil and Peggy are walking on the beach and come across it. Phil leans down and picks it up. Phil opens the bottle and pulls out the note. He starts to read it out loud to Peggy.

Phil reads, "Mom, Dad. I love you, and I miss you so much. Thank you for everything. I hope Rachel and I can have the same love that you shared. Say hi to Travis from all of us."

Phil and Peggy continue walking on the beach over to Travis, who is sitting next to a couple of empty lawn chairs, looking out over the ocean. Travis hands a beer to Phil.

Travis asks Phil, "Everything okay?"

Phil replies, "I think so. Brad wanted to tell you hi from everybody."

Travis says, "I'm glad Brad is going to be there for PJ."